Arabian Nights

Arabian Nights

Stories Told by Scheherazade

retold by
Laurence Housman

with illustrations by
Edmund Dulac

Abaris Books · New York

International Standard Book Number 0-913870-91-9
This book has been entirely reset in Palatino type.
New edition first published in 1981 by Abaris Books, Inc.
24 West 40th Street, New York, NY 10018
Printed in the United States of America
Second printing 1983

Book design: Ken Meads
Story selection and arrangement: Lisa Roth

CONTENTS

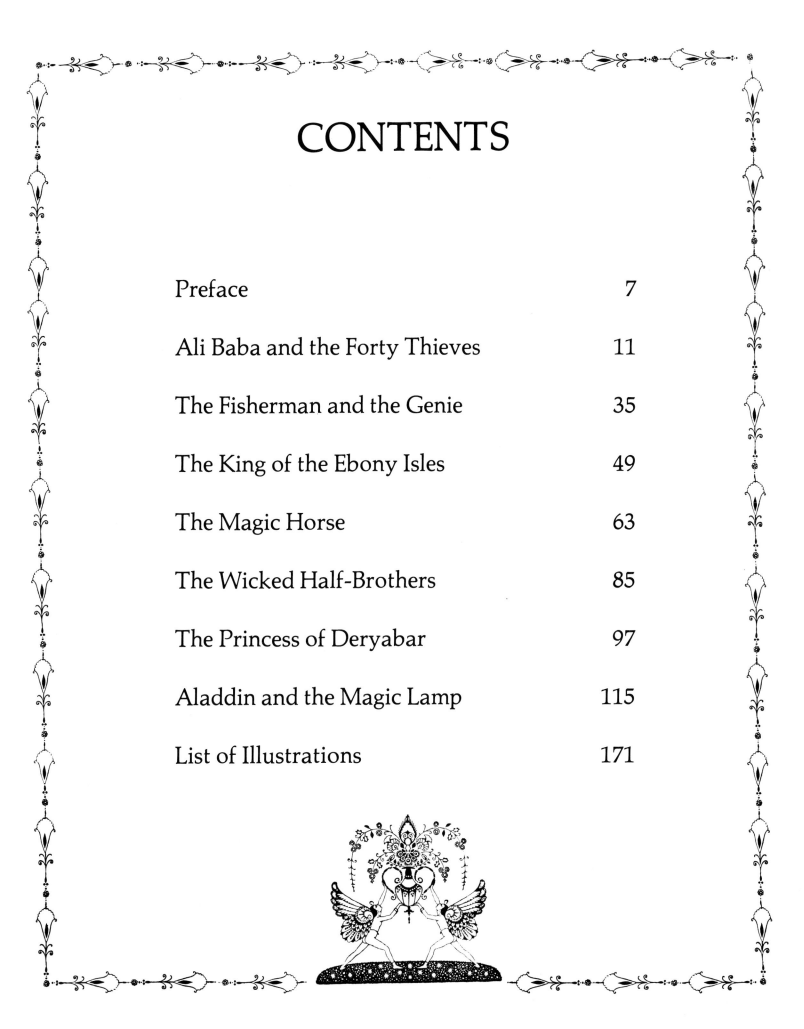

PREFACE

Scheherazade, the heroine of *The Thousand and One Nights*, ranks among the great storytellers of the world much as does Penelope among the weavers. Enchanting a wicked king with her crafty tales she turned him away from his murderous intentions. Procrastination was the basis of her art; for though the task she accomplished was splendid and memorable, it is rather in the quantity than the quality of her invention—in the long spun-out performance of what could have been done far more shortly—that she becomes a figure of dramatic interest. The idea which binds the stories together is greater and more romantic than the stories themselves; and though, both in the original and in translation, the diurnal interruption of their flows is more and more taken for granted, we are never quite robbed of the sense that it is Scheherazade who is speaking—Scheherazade, loquacious and self-possessed, sitting up in bed at the renewed call of dawn to save her neck for the round of another day. Here is a figure of romance worth a dozen of the prolix stories to which it has been made sponsor; and often we may have followed the fortunes of some shoddy hero and heroine chiefly to determine at what possible point of interest the narrator could have left hanging that frail thread on which for another twenty-four hours her life was to depend.

Yes, the idea is delightful; and, with the fiction of Scheherazade to color them, the tales acquire a rank which they would not otherwise deserve; their prolixity is then the crowning point of their art, their sententious truisms have a flavor of ironic wit, their repetitions become humorous, their trivialities a mark of lighthearted courage; even those deeper indiscretions, which Burton has so faithfully recorded, seem then but a wise adaptation of vile means to a noble end. And yet we know that it is not so; for, as a matter

of fact, *The Arabian Nights Entertainment* is but a miscellany gathered from various sources, of various dates, and passing down to us, even in its collocated form, under widely differing versions. None but scholars can know how little of the unadulterated originals has come into our possession; and only those whose pious opinions shut their eyes to obvious facts can object in principle to the simplification of a form which, from the point of view of mere storytelling, can so easily be bettered. Even the more accurate of the versions ordinarily available are full of abridgement, alteration, and suppression; and if you have to eliminate Scheherazade and select your stories mainly with a view to illustration, then you have very largely done away with the reasons for treating tenderly that prolixity which in an impatient age tends to debar readers from an old classic.

And so, in the present version, whoever shall care to make comparison will find that the original material has been treated with considerable freedom in the direction of brevity, and with an almost uniform departure from the exact text, save where essentials of plot or character or local color required a closer accuracy. In the case also of conflicting versions, there has been no reluctance to choose and combine in order to secure a livelier result; and a further freedom has sometimes been taken of giving to an incident more meaning and connection that has been allowed to it in the original. That is, perhaps, the greatest licence of all, but it is the one that does least harm in formal result; for no one can read the majority of the tales in their accepted versions without perceiving that, as regards construction and the piecing of event with event, they are either incredibly careless or discreditably perfunctory.

But because they contain, though at a low pressure, the expression of so much life, habit and custom, so many colored and secluded interiors, so quaint a commingling of crowds, so brilliant and moving a pageantry of

Eastern mediaevalism, because of all these things *The Arabian Nights* will still retain their perennial charm. Those of us who read are all travellers; and never is our travelling sense so awakened perhaps, as when we dip into a book such as this where the incredible and the commonplace are so curiously blended, and where Genie and Efrite and Magician have far less interest for us now than the silly staring crowds, and the bobbing camels in the narrow streets, and Scheherazade spinning her poor thin yarn of wonders that she may share for another night the pillow of a homicidal maniac.

Although we cannot be quite certain, the collection of stories, *The Thousand and One Nights* is principally of Persian origin. The tale of Scheherazade is mentioned by Mas'udi as early as A.D. 944. Yet some of the stories seem more Arabic than Persian in character.

They were translated into French by Antoine Galland between 1704 and 1712. Several translations of selected stories into English followed, the most notable among them the one by Edwin William Lane, published in 1840. The first "full, complete, uncastrated" version appeared in ten volumes 1885/86, translated by Sir Richard Francis Burton (1821-1890), an expert Arabist and one-time British consul at Damascus. Six supplementary volumes followed in 1887/88. Sold on subscription basis, the high price of this edition limited its circulation, and, as we now know, by volition on the part of the author. *The Arabian Nights*, as retold by Laurence Housman, first appeared in 1907.

The present edition can only serve to introduce the reader to the flights of imagination of the authors of these tales, as well as to the delight to the eye, due to the artistry of the author of the illustrations, Edmund Dulac.

ALI BABA AND THE
FORTY THIEVES

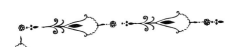 

IN a town in Persia lived two brothers named Cassim and Ali Baba, between whom their father at his death had left what little property he possessed equally divided. Cassim, however, having married the heiress of a rich merchant, became soon after his marriage the owner of a fine shop, together with several pieces of land, and was in consequence, through no effort of his own, the most considerable merchant in the town. Ali Baba, on the other hand, was married to one as poor as himself, and having no other means of gaining a livelihood he used to go every day into the forest to cut wood, and lading therewith the three asses which were his sole stock-in-trade, would then hawk it about the streets for sale.

One day while he was at work within the skirts of the forest, Ali Baba saw advancing towards him across the open a large company of horsemen, and fearing from their appearance that they might be robbers, he left his asses to their own devices and sought safety for himself in the lower branches of a large tree which grew in the close overshadowing of a precipitous rock.

Almost immediately it became evident that this very rock was the goal toward which the troop was bound, for having arrived they alighted instantly from their horses, and took down each man of them a sack which seemed by its weight and form to be filled with gold. There could no longer be any doubt that they were robbers. Ali Baba counted forty of them.

Just as he had done so, the one nearest to him, who seemed to be their chief, advanced toward the rock, and in a low but distinct voice uttered the two words, "Open Sesamé!" Immediately the rock opened like a door, the captain and his men passed in, and the rock closed behind them.

For a long while Ali Baba waited, not daring to descend from his hiding place lest they should come out and catch him in the act; but at last, when the waiting had grown almost unbearable, his patience was rewarded, the door in the rock opened, and out came the forty men, their captain leading them.

When the last of them was through, "Shut, Sesamé!" said the captain, and immediately the face of the rock closed together as before. Then they all mounted their horses and rode away.

As soon as he felt sure that they were not returning Ali Baba came down from the tree and made his way at once to that part of the rock where he had seen the captain and his men enter. And there at the words "Open, Sesamé!" a door suddenly revealed itself and opened.

Ali Baba had expected to find a dark and gloomy cavern. Great was his astonishment therefore when he perceived a spacious and vaulted chamber lighted from above through a fissure in the rock; and there spread out before him lay treasures in profusion, bales of merchandise, silks, carpets, brocades, and above all gold and silver lying in loose heaps or in sacks piled one upon another. He did not take long to consider what he should do. Disregarding the silver and the gold that lay loose, he brought to the mouth of the cave as many sacks of gold as he thought his three asses might carry; and having loaded them on and covered them with wood so that they might not be seen, he closed the rock by the utterance of the magic words which he had learned, and departed for the town, a well-satisfied man.

When he got home he drove his asses into a small court, and shutting the gates carefully he took off the wood that covered the bags and carried them in to his wife. She, discovering them to be full of gold, feared that her husband had stolen them, and began sorrowfully to reproach him; but Ali Baba soon put her mind at rest on that score, and having poured all the gold into a great heap upon the floor he sat down at her side to consider how well it looked.

Soon his wife, poor careful body, must needs begin counting it over piece by piece. Ali Baba let her go on for awhile, but before long the sight set him laughing. "Wife," said he, "you will never make an end of it that way. The best thing to do is to dig a hole and bury it, then we shall be sure that it is not slipping through our fingers." "That will do well enough," said his wife," but it

would be better first to have the measure of it. So while you dig the hole I will go round to Cassim's and borrow a measure small enough to give us an exact reckoning. "Do as you will," answered her husband, "but see that you keep the thing secret."

Off went Ali Baba's wife to her brother-in-law's house. Cassim was away from home, so she begged of his wife the loan of a small measure, naming for choice the smallest. This set the sister-in-law wondering. Knowing Ali Baba's poverty she was all the more curious to find out for what kind of grain so small a measure could be needed. So before bringing it she covered all the bottom with lard, and giving it to Ali Baba's wife told her to be sure and be quick in returning it. The other, promising to restore it punctually, made haste to get home; and there finding the hole dug for its reception she started to measure the money into it. First she set the measure upon the heap, then she filled it, then she carried it to the hole; and so she continued till the last measure was counted. Then, leaving Ali Baba to finish the burying, she carried back the measure with all haste to her sister-in-law, returning thanks for the loan.

No sooner was her back turned than Cassim's wife looked at the bottom of the measure, and there to her astonishment she saw sticking to the lard a gold coin. "What?" she cried, her heart filled with envy, "Is Ali Baba so rich that he needs a measure for his gold? Where, then, may I know, has the miserable wretch obtained it?"

She waited with impatience for her husband's return, and as soon as he came in she began to jeer at him. "You think yourself rich," said she, "but Ali Baba is richer. You count your gold by the piece, but Ali Baba does not count, he measures it! In comparison to Ali Baba we are but grubs and groundlings!"

Having thus riddled him to the top of her bent in order to provoke his curiosity, she told him the story of the borrowed measure, of her own stratagem, and of its result.

Cassim, instead of being pleased at Ali Baba's sudden prosperity, grew furiously jealous; not a wink could he sleep all night for thinking of it. The next morning before sunrise he went to his brother's house. "Ali Baba," said he, "what do you mean by pretending to be poor when all the time you are scooping up gold by the quart?" "Brother," said Ali Baba, "explain your meaning." "My meaning shall be plain!" cried Cassim, displaying the tell-tale coin. "How many more pieces have you like this that my wife found sticking to the bottom of the measure yesterday?"

Ali Baba, perceiving that the intervention of wives had made further concealment useless, told his brother the true facts of the case, and offered him, as an inducement for keeping the secret, an equal share of the treasure.

"That is the least that I have the right to expect," answered Cassim haughtily. "It is further necessary that you should tell me exactly where the treasure lies, that I may, if need be, test the truth of your story, otherwise I shall find it my duty to denounce you to the authorities."

Ali Baba, having a clear conscience, had little fear of Cassim's threats but out of pure good nature he gave him all the information he desired, not forgetting to instruct him in the words which would give him free passage into the cave and out again.

Cassim, who had thus secured all he had come for, lost no time in putting his project into execution. Intent on possessing himself of all the treasures which yet remained, he set off the next morning before daybreak, taking with him ten mules laden with empty crates. Arrived before the cave, he recalled the words which his brother had taught him; no sooner was "Open Sesamé!" said than the door in the rock lay wide for him to pass through, and when he had entered it shut again.

If the simple soul of Ali Baba had found delight in the riches of the cavern, greater still was the exultation of a greedy nature like Cassim's. Intoxicated with the wealth that lay before his eyes, he had no thought but to gather together with all speed as much treasure as the ten mules could carry; and so,

having exhausted himself with heavy labor and avaricious excitement, he suddenly found on returning to the door that he had forgotten the key which opened it. Up and down, and in and out through the mazes of his brain he chased the missing word. Barley, and maize, and rice, he thought of them all: but of sesamé never once, because his mind had become dark to the revealing light of heaven. And so the door stayed fast, holding him prisoner in the cave, where to his fate, undeserving of pity, we leave him.

Toward noon the robbers returned, and saw, standing about the rock, the ten mules laden with crates. At this they were greatly surprised, and began to search with suspicion amongst the surrounding crannies and undergrowth. Finding no one there, they drew their swords and advanced cautiously toward the cave, where, upon the captain's pronouncement of the magic word, the door immediately fell open. Cassim, who from within had heard the trampling of horses, had now no doubt that the robbers had arrived and that his hour had come. Resolved however to make one last effort at escape, he stood ready by the door; and no sooner had the opening word been uttered than he sprang forth with such violence that he threw the captain to the ground. But his attempt was vain; before he could break through he was mercilessly hacked down by the swords of the robber band.

With their fears thus verified, the robbers anxiously entered the cave to view the traces of its late visitant. There they saw piled by the door the treasure which Cassim had sought to carry away; but while restoring this to its place they failed altogether to detect the earlier loss which Ali Baba had caused them. Reckoning, however, that as one had discovered the secret of entry others also might know of it, they determined to leave an example for any who might venture thither on a similar errand; and having quartered the body of Cassim they disposed it at the entrance in a manner most calculated to strike horror into the heart of the beholder. Then, closing the door of the cave, they rode away in search of fresh exploits and plunder.

Meanwhile Cassim's wife had grown very uneasy at her husband's prolonged absence; and at nightfall, unable to endure further suspense, she ran to Ali Baba, and telling him of his brother's secret expedition, entreated him to go out instantly in search of him.

Ali Baba had too kind a heart to refuse or delay comfort to her affliction. Taking with him his three asses he set out immediately for the forest, and as the road was familiar to him he had soon found his way to the door of the cave. When he saw there the traces of blood he became filled with misgiving, but no sooner had he entered than his worst fears were realized. Nevertheless brotherly piety gave him courage. Gathering together the severed remains and wrapping them about with all possible decency, he laid them upon one of the asses; then bethinking him that he deserved some payment for his pains, he loaded the two remaining asses with sacks of gold, and covering them with wood as on the first occasion, made his way back to the town while it was yet early. Leaving his wife to dispose of the treasure borne by the two asses, he led the third to his sister-in-law's house, and knocking quietly so that none of the neighbors might hear, was presently admitted by Morgiana, a female slave whose intelligence and discretion had long been known to him. "Morgiana," said he, "there's trouble on the back of that ass. Can you keep a secret?" And Morgiana's nod satisfied him better than any oath. "Well," said he, "your master's body lies there waiting to be pieced, and our business now is to bury him honorably as though he had died a natural death. Go and tell your mistress that I want to speak to her."

Morgiana went in to her mistress, and returning presently bade Ali Baba enter. Then leaving him to break to his sister-in-law the news and the sad circumstances of his brother's death, she, with her plan already formed, hastened forth and knocked at the door of the nearest apothecary. As soon as he opened to her she required of him in trembling agitation certain pillules efficacious against grave disorders, declaring in answer to his questions that her master had been taken suddenly ill. With these she returned home, and

her plan of concealment having been explained and agreed upon, much to the satisfaction of Ali Baba, she went forth the next morning to the same apothecary, and with tears in her eyes besought him to supply her in haste with a certain drug that is given to sick people only in the last extremity. Meanwhile the rumor of Cassim's sickness had got abroad; Ali Baba and his wife had been seen coming and going, while Morgiana by her ceaseless activity had made the two days' pretended illness seem like a fortnight. So when a sound of wailing arose within the house all the neighbors concluded without further question that Cassim had died a natural and honorable death.

But Morgiana had now a still more difficult task to perform, it being necessary for the obsequies that the body should be made in some way presentable. So at a very early hour the next morning she went to the shop of a certain merry old cobbler, Baba Mustapha by name, who lived on the other side of town. Showing him a piece of gold she inquired whether he were ready to earn it by exercising his craft in implicit obedience to her instructions. And when Baba Mustapha sought to know the terms, "First," said she, "you must come with your eyes bandaged; secondly, you must sew what I put before you without asking questions; and thirdly, when you return you must tell nobody."

Mustapha, who had a lively curiosity into other folk's affairs, boggled for a time at the bandaging, and doubted much of his ability to refrain from question; but having on these considerations secured the doubling of his fee, he promised secrecy readily enough, and taking his cobbler's tackle in hand submitted himself to Morgiana's guidance and set forth. This way and that she led him blindfold, till she had brought him to the house of her deceased master. Then uncovering his eyes in the presence of the dismembered corpse, she bade him get out thread and wax and join the pieces together.

Baba Mustapha plied his task according to the compact, asking no question. When he had done, Morgiana again bandaged his eyes and led him home, and giving him a third piece of gold the more to satisfy him, she bade him good-day and departed.

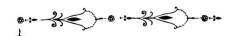

So in seemliness and without scandal of any kind were the obsequies of the murdered Cassim performed. And when all was ended, seeing that his widow was desolate and his house in need of a protector, Ali Baba with brotherly piety took both the one and the other into his care, marrying his sister-in-law according to Moslem rule, and removing with all his goods and newly acquired treasure to the house which had been his brother's. And having also acquired the shop where Cassim had done business, he put into it his own son, who had already served an apprenticeship to the trade. So, with his fortune well established, let us now leave Ali Baba, and return to the robber's cave.

Thither, at the appointed time, came the forty robbers, bearing in hand fresh booty; and great was their consternation to discover that not only had the body of Cassim been removed, but a good many sacks of gold as well. It was no wonder that this should trouble them, for so long as anyone could command secret access, the cave was useless as a depository for their wealth. The question was, "What could they do to put an end to their present insecurity?" After long debate it was agreed that one of their number should go into the town disguised as a traveller, and there, mixing with the common people, learn from their report whether there had been recently any case in their midst of sudden prosperity or sudden death. If such a thing could be discovered, then they made sure of tracking the evil to its source and imposing a remedy.

Although the penalty for failure was death, one of the robbers at once boldly offered himself for the venture, and having transformed himself by disguise and received the wise counsels and commendations of his fellows, he set out for the town.

Arriving at dawn he began to walk up and down the streets and watch the early stirring of the inhabitants. So, before long, he drew up at the door of Baba Mustapha, who, though old, was already seated at work upon his cobbler's bench. The robber accosted him. "I wonder," said he, "to see a man

Their chief in a low but distinct voice
uttered the two words "Open Sesamé!"

of your age at work so early. Does not so dull a light strain your eyes?" "Not so much as you might think," answered Baba Mustapha. "Why, it was but the other day that at this same hour I saw well enough to stitch up a dead body in a place where it was certainly no lighter." "Stitch up a dead body!" cried the robber in pretended amazement, concealing his joy at this sudden intelligence. "Surely you mean in its winding sheet, for how else can a dead body be stitched?" "No, no," said Mustapha; "what I say I mean; but as it is a secret, I can tell you no more." The robber drew out a piece of gold. "Come," said he, "tell me nothing you do not care to; only show me the house where lay the body that you stitched." Baba Mustapha eyed the gold longingly. "Would that I could," he replied; "but alas! I went to it blindfold." "Well," said the robber, "I have heard that a blind man remembers his road; perhaps, though seeing you might lose it, blindfold you might find it again." Tempted by the offer of a second piece of gold, Baba Mustapha was soon persuaded to make the attempt. "It was here that I started," said he, showing the spot, "and I turned as you see me now." The robber then put a bandage over his eyes, and walked beside him through the streets, partly guiding and partly being led, till of his own accord Baba Mustapha stopped. "It was here," said he. "The door by which I went in should now lie to the right." And he had in fact come exactly opposite to the house which had once been Cassim's, where Ali Baba now dwelt.

The robber, having marked the door with a piece of chalk which he had provided for the purpose, removed the bandage from Mustapha's eyes, and leaving him to his own devices returned with all possible speed to the cave where his comrades were awaiting him.

Soon after the robber and cobbler had parted, Morgiana happened to go out upon an errand, and as she returned she noticed the mark upon the door. "This," she thought, "is not as it should be; either some trick is intended, or there is evil brewing for my master's house." Taking a piece of chalk she put a similar mark upon the five or six doors lying to right and left; and having done this she went home with her mind satisfied, saying nothing.

In the meantime the robbers had learned from their companion the success of his venture. Greatly elated at the thought of the vengeance so soon to be theirs, they formed a plan for entering the city in a manner that should arouse no suspicion among the inhabitants. Passing in by twos and threes, and by different routes, they came together to the market-place at an appointed time, while the captain and the robber who had acted as spy made their way alone to the street in which the marked door was to be found. Presently, just as they had expected, they perceived a door with the mark on it. "That is it!" said the robber; but as they continued walking so as to avoid suspicion, they came upon another and another, till, before they were done, they had passed six in succession. So alike were the marks that the spy, though he swore he had made but one, could not tell which it was. Seeing that the design had failed, the captain returned to the market-place, and having passed the word for his troop to go back in the same way as they had come, he himself set the example of retreat.

When they were all reassembled in the forest, the captain explained how the matter had fallen, and the spy, acquiescing in his own condemnation, kneeled down and received the stroke of the executioner.

But as it was still necessary for the safety of all that so great a trespass and theft should not pass unavenged, another of the band, undeterred by the fate of his comrade, volunteered upon the same conditions to prosecute the quest wherein the other had failed. Coming by the same means to the house of Ali Baba, he set upon the door, at a spot not likely to be noticed, a mark in red chalk to distinguish it clearly from those which were already marked in white. But even this precaution failed of its end. Morgiana, whose eye nothing could escape, noticed the red mark at the first time of passing, and dealt with it just as she had done with the previous one. So when the robbers came, hoping this time to light upon the door without fail, they found not one but six all similarly marked with red.

*She poured into each jar in turn a sufficient quantity
of the boiling oil to scald its occupant to death*

When the second spy had received the due reward of his blunder, the captain considered how by trusting to others he had come to lose two of his bravest followers, so the third attempt he determined to conduct in person. Having found his way to Ali Baba's door, as the two others had done by the aid of Baba Mustapha, he did not set any mark upon it, but examined it so carefully that he could not in future mistake it. He then returned to the forest and communicated to his band the plan which he had formed. This was to go into town in the disguise of an oil-merchant, bearing with him upon the nineteen mules thirty-eight large leather jars, one of which, as a sample, was to be full of oil, but all the others empty. In these he purposed to conceal the thirty-seven robbers to which his band was now reduced, and so to convey his full force to the scene of action in such a manner as to arouse no suspicion till the signal for vengeance should be given.

Within a couple of days he had secured all the mules and jars that were requisite, and having disposed of his troop according to the pre-arranged plan, he drove his train of well-laden mules to the gates of the city, through which he passed just before sunset. Proceeding thence to Ali Baba's house, and arriving as it fell dark, he was about to knock and crave a lodging for the night, when he perceived Ali Baba at the door enjoying the fresh air after supper. Addressing him in tones of respect, "Sir," said he, "I have brought my oil a great distance to sell tomorrow in the market; and at this late hour, being a stranger, I know not where to seek for a shelter. If it is not troubling you too much, allow me to stable my beasts here for the night."

The captain's voice was now so changed from its accustomed tone of command, that Ali Baba, though he had heard it before, did not recognize it. Not only did he grant the stranger's request for bare accommodation, but as soon as the unlading and stabling of the mules had been accomplished, he invited him to stay no longer in the outer court but enter the house as his guest. The captain, whose plans this proposal somewhat disarranged, endeavoured to excuse himself from a pretended reluctance to give trouble;

but since Ali Baba would take no refusal he was forced at last to yield, and to submit with apparent complaisance to an entertainment which the hospitality of his host extended to a late hour.

When they were about to retire for the night, Ali Baba went into the kitchen to speak to Morgiana; and the captain of the robbers, on the pretext of going to look after his mules, slipped out into the yard where the oil-jars were standing in line. Passing from jar to jar he whispered into each, "When you hear a handful of pebbles fall from the window of the chamber where I am lodged, then cut your way out of the jar and make ready, for the time will have come." He then returned to the house, where Morgiana came with a light and conducted him to his chamber.

Now Ali Baba, before going to bed, had said to Morgiana, "Tomorrow at dawn I am going to the baths; let my bathing-linen be put ready, and see that the cook has some good broth prepared for me against my return." Having therefore led the guest up to his chamber, Morgiana returned to the kitchen and ordered Abdallah the cook to put on the pot for the broth. Suddenly while she was skimming it, the lamp went out, and, on searching, she found there was no more oil in the house. At so late an hour no shop would be open, yet somehow the broth had to be made, and that could not be done without a light. "As for that," said Abdallah, seeing her perplexity, "why trouble yourself? There is plenty of oil out in the yard." "Why, to be sure!" said Morgiana, and sending Abdallah to bed so that he might be up in time to wake his master on the morrow, she took the oil-can herself and went out into the court. As she approached the jar which stood nearest, she heard a voice within say, "Is it time?"

To one of Morgiana's intelligence an oil-jar that spoke was an object of even more suspicion than a chalk-mark on a door, and in an instant she apprehended what danger for her master and his family might lie concealed around her. Understanding well enough that an oil-jar which asked a question required an answer, she replied quick as thought and without the

least sign of perturbation, "Not yet, but presently." And thus she passed from jar to jar, thirty-seven in all, giving the same answer, till she came to the one which contained the oil.

The situation was now clear to her. Aware of the source from which her master had acquired his wealth, she guessed at once that, in extending shelter to the oil-merchant, Ali Baba had in fact admitted to his house the robber captain and his band. On the instant her resolution was formed. Having filled the oil-can she returned to the kitchen; there she lighted the lamp and then, taking a large kettle, went back once more to the jar which contained the oil. Filling the kettle she carried it back to the kitchen, and putting under it a great fire of wood had soon brought it to the boil. Then taking it in hand once more, she went out into the yard and poured into each jar in turn a sufficient quantity of the boiling oil to scald its occupant to death.

She then returned to the kitchen, and having made Ali Baba's broth, put out the fire, blew out the lamp, and sat down by the window to watch.

Before long the captain of the robbers awoke from the short sleep which he had allowed himself, and finding that all was silent in the house, he rose softly and opened the window. Below stood the oil-jars; gently into their midst he threw the handful of pebbles agreed on as a signal; but from the oil-jars came no answer. He threw a second and a third time; yet though he could hear the pebbles falling among the jars, there followed only the silence of the dead. Wondering whether his band had fled leaving him in the lurch, or whether they were all asleep, he grew uneasy, and descending in haste, made his way into the court. As he approached the first jar a smell of burning and hot oil assailed his nostrils, and looking within he beheld in rigid contortion the dead body of his comrade. In every jar the same sight presented itself, till he came to the one which had contained the oil. There, in what was missing, the means and manner of his companions' death were made clear to him. Aghast at the discovery and awake to the danger that now threatened him, he did not delay an instant, but forcing the garden-gate, and thence climbing from wall to wall, he made his escape out of the city.

When Morgiana, who had remained all this time on the watch, was assured of his final departure, she put her master's bath-linen ready and went to bed well satisfied with her day's work.

The next morning Ali Baba, awakened by his slave, went to the baths before daybreak. On his return he was greatly surprised to find that the merchant was gone, leaving his mules and oil-jars behind him. He inquired of Morgiana the reason. "You will find the reason," said she, "if you look into the first jar you come to." Ali Baba did so, and, seeing a man, started back with a cry. "Do not be afraid," said Morgiana, "he is dead and harmless; and so are all the others whom you will find if you look further."

As Ali Baba went from one jar to another, finding always the same sight of horror within, his knees trembled under him; and when he came at last to the one empty oil-jar, he stood for a time motionless, turning upon Morgiana eyes of wonder and inquiry. "And what," he said then, "has become of the merchant?" "To tell you that," said Morgiana, "will be to tell you the whole story; you will be better able to hear it if you have your broth first."

But the curiosity of Ali Baba was far too great: he would not be kept waiting. So without further delay she gave him the whole history, so far as she knew it, from beginning to end; and by her intelligent putting of one thing against another, she left him at last in no possible doubt as to the source and nature of the conspiracy which her quick wits had so happily defeated. "And now, dear master," she said in conclusion, "continue to be on your guard, for though all these are dead, one remains alive; and he, if I mistake not, is the captain of the band, and for that reason the more formidable and the more likely to cherish the hope of vengeance."

When Morgiana had done speaking Ali Baba clearly perceived that he owed to her not merely the protection of his property but life itself. His heart was full of gratitude. "Do not doubt," he said, "that before I die I will reward you as you deserve; and as an immediate proof from this moment I give you your liberty."

This token of his approval filled Morgiana's heart with delight, but she had no intention of leaving so kind a master, even had she been sure that all danger was now over. The immediate question which next presented itself was how to dispose of the bodies. Luckily at the far end of the garden stood a thick grove of trees, and under these Ali Baba was able to dig a large trench without attracting the notice of his neighbors. Here the remains of the thirty-seven robbers were laid side by side, the trench was filled again, and the ground made level. As for the mules, since Ali Baba had no use for them, he sent them, one or two at a time, to the market to be sold.

Meanwhile the robber captain had fled back to the forest. Entering the cave he was overcome by its gloom and loneliness. "Alas!" he cried, "my comrades, partners in my adventures, sharers of my fortune, how shall I endure to live without you? Why did I lead you to a fate where valour was of no avail, and where death turned you into objects of ridicule? Surely had you died sword in hand my sorrow had been less bitter! And now what remains for me but to take vengeance for your death and to prove, by achieving it without aid, that I was worthy to be the captain of such a band!"

Thus resolved, at an early hour the next day, he assumed a disguise suitable to his purpose, and going to the town took lodging in a khan. Entering into conversation with his host he inquired whether anything of interest had happened recently in the town; but the other, though full of gossip, had nothing to tell him concerning the matter in which he was most interested, for Ali Baba, having to conceal from all the source of his wealth, had also to be silent as to the dangers in which it involved him.

The captain then inquired where there was a shop for hire; and hearing of one that suited him, he came to terms with the owner, and before long had furnished it with all kinds of rich stuffs and carpets and jewelry which he brought by degrees with great secrecy from the cave.

Now this shop happened to be opposite to that which had belonged to Cassim and was now occupied by the son of Ali Baba; so before long the son

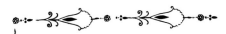

and the newcomer, who had assumed the name of Cogia Houssain, became acquainted; and as the youth had good looks, kind manners, and a sociable disposition, it was not long before the acquaintance became intimate.

Cogia Houssain did all he could to seal the pretended friendship, the more so as it had not taken him long to discover how the young man and Ali Baba were related; so, plying him constantly wth small presents and acts of hospitality, he forced on him the obligation of making some return.

Ali Baba's son, however, had not at his lodging sufficient accommodation for entertainment; he therefore told his father of the difficulty in which Cogia Houssain's favors had placed him, and Ali Baba with great willingness at once offered to arrange matters. "My son," said he, "tomorrow being a holiday, all shops will be closed; then do you after dinner invite Cogia Houssain to walk with you; and as you return bring him this way and beg him to come in. That will be better than a formal invitation, and Morgiana shall have a supper prepared for you."

This proposal was exactly what Ali Baba's son could have wished, so on the morrow he brought Cogia Houssain to the door as if by accident, and stopping, invited him to enter.

Cogia Houssain, who saw his object thus suddenly attained, began by showing pretended reluctance, but Ali Baba himself coming to the door, pressed him in the most kindly manner to enter, and before long had conducted him to the table, where food stood prepared.

But there an unlooked-for difficulty arose. Wicked though he might be, the robber captain was not so impious as to eat the salt of the man he intended to kill. He therefore began with many apologies to excuse himself; and when Ali Baba sought to know the reason, "Sir," said he, "I am sure that if you knew the cause of my resolution you would approve of it. Suffice it to say that I have made it a rule to eat of no dish that has salt in it. How then can I sit down at your table if I must reject everything that is set before me?"

"If that is your scruple," said Ali Baba, "it shall soon be satisfied," and he sent orders to the kitchen that no salt was to be put into any of the dishes

served to the newly arrived guest. "Thus," said he to Cogia Houssain, "I shall still have the honor, to which I have looked forward, of returning to you under my own roof the hospitality you have shown to my son."

Morgiana, who was just about to serve supper, received the order with some discontent. "Who," she said, "is this difficult person that refuses to eat salt? He must be a curiosity worth looking at." So when the saltless courses were ready to be set upon the table, she herself helped to carry in the dishes. No sooner had she set eyes on Cogia Houssain than she recognized him in spite of his disguise; and observing his movements with great attention she saw that he had a dagger concealed beneath his robe. "Ah!" she said to herself, "here is reason enough! For who will eat salt with the man he means to murder? But he shall not murder my master if I can prevent it."

Now Morgiana knew that the most favorable opportunity for the robber captain to carry out his design would be after the courses had been withdrawn, and when Ali Baba and his son and guest were alone together over their wine, which indeed was the very project that Cogia Houssain had formed. Going forth, therefore, in haste, she dressed herself as a dancer, assuming the headdress and mask suitable for the character. Then she fastened a silver girdle about her waist, and hung upon it a dagger of the same material. Thus equipped, she said to Abdallah the cook, "Take your tabor and let us go in and give an entertainment in honor of our master's guest."

So Abdallah took his tabor, and played Morgiana into the hall. As soon as she had entered she made a low curtsy, and stood awaiting orders. Then Ali Baba, seeing that she wished to perform in his guest's honor, said kindly, "Come in, Morgiana, and show Cogia Houssain what you can do."

Immediately Abdallah began to beat upon his tabor and sing an air for Morgiana to dance to; and she, advancing with much grace and propriety of deportment, began to move through several figures, performing them with

the ease and facility which none but the most highly practiced can attain to. Then, for the last figure of all, she drew out the dagger and, holding it in her hand, danced a dance which excelled all that had preceded it in the surprise and change and quickness and dexterity of its movements. Now she presented the dagger at her own breast, now at one of the onlookers; but always in the act of striking she drew back. At length, as though out of breath, she snatched his instrument from Abdallah with her left hand, and, still holding the dagger in her right, advanced the hollow of the tabor toward her master, as is the custom of dancers when claiming their fee. Ali Baba threw in a piece of gold; his son did likewise. Then advancing it in the same manner toward Cogia Houssain, who was feeling for his purse, she struck under it, and before he knew had plunged her dagger deep into his heart.

Ali Baba and his son, seeing their guest fall dead, cried out in horror at the deed. "Wretch!" exclaimed Ali Baba, "what ruin and shame hast thou brought on us?" "Nay," answered Morgiana, "it is not your ruin but your life that I have thus secured; look and convince yourself what man was this which refused to eat salt with you!" So saying, she tore off the dead robber's disguise, showing the dagger concealed below, and the face which her master now for the first time recognized.

Ali Baba's gratitude to Morgiana for thus preserving his life a second time, knew no bounds. He took her in his arms and embraced her as a daughter. "Now," said he, "the time is come when I must fulfill my debt; and how better can I do it than by marrying you to my son?" This proposition, far from proving unwelcome to the young man, did but confirm an inclination already formed. A few days later the nuptials were celebrated with great joy and solemnity, and the union thus auspiciously commenced was productive of as much happiness as lies within the power of mortals to secure.

As for the robber's cave, it remained the secret possession of Ali Baba and his posterity; and using their good fortune with equity and moderation, they rose to high office in the city and were held in great honor by all who knew them.

THE FISHERMAN
AND THE GENIE

 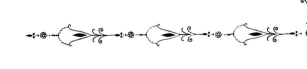

THERE was once an old fisherman who lived in great poverty with a wife and three children. But though poorer than others he ever toiled in humble submission to the decrees of Providence, and so, at the same hour each day, he would cast his net four times into the sea, and whatever it brought up to him therewith he rested content.

One day, having cast for the first time, he found his net so heavy that he could scarcely draw it in; yet when at last he got it to shore all that it contained was the carcass of an ass.

He cast a second time, and found the draught of the net even heavier than before. But again he was doomed to disappointment, for this time it contained nothing but a large earthenware jar full of mud and sand. His third attempt brought him only a heap of broken old bottles and potsherds: fortune seemed to be against him. Then, committing his hope to Providence, he cast for the fourth and last time; and once more the weight of the net was so great that he was unable to haul it. When at last he got it to land, he found that it contained a brazen vessel, its mouth closed with a leaden stopper, bearing upon it the seal of King Solomon.

The sight cheered him. "This," thought he, "I can sell in the market, where I may get for it enough to buy a measure of corn; and, if one is to judge by weight, what lies within may prove yet more valuable."

Thus reckoning, he pried out the stopper with his knife, and turning the vessel upside down looked for the contents to follow. Great was his astonishment when nothing but smoke came out of it. The smoke rose in a thick black column and spread like a mist between earth and sky, till presently, drawing together, it took form; and there in its midst stood a mighty Genie, whose brows touched heaven while his feet rested upon ground. His head was like a dome, his hands were like flails, and his legs like pine trees; his mouth was black as a cavern, his nostrils were like trumpets, his eyes blazed like torches, and his wings whirled round and over him like the simoom of the desert.

At so fearful a sight all the fisherman's courage oozed out of him; but the Genie, perceiving him, cried with a loud voice, "O Solomon, Prophet of God, slay me not, for never again will I withstand thee in word or deed."

"Alas!" said the fisherman, "I am no prophet; and as for Solomon, he has been dead for nearly two thousand years. I am but a poor fisherman whom chance has knocked by accident against thy door."

"In that case," answered the Genie, "know that presently thou wilt have to die."

"Heaven forbid!" cried the fisherman; "or, at least, tell me why! Surely it might seem that I had done thee some service in releasing thee."

"Hear first my story," said the Genie, "then shalt thou understand."

"Well, if I must!" said the fisherman, resigning himself to the inevitable; "but make it short, for truly I have small stomach left in me now for the hearing of tales."

"Know, then," said the Genie, "that I am one of those spirits which resisted the power and dominion of Solomon; and when, having brought into submission all the rest of my race, he could not make me yield to him either reverence or service, he caused me to be shut up in this bottle, and sealing it with his own seal cast it down into the depths of the sea.

"Now when I had lain there prisoner for a hundred years, I swore in my heart that I would give to the man that should release me all the treasures attainable in heaven or earth. But when none came to earn so great a reward in all the hundred years that followed, then I swore that I would give to my liberator earthly riches only; and when this gift also had lain despised for yet another hundred years, then would I promise no more than the fulfillment of three wishes. But thereafter finding that all promises and vows were vain, my heart became consumed with rage, and I swore by Allah that I would only grant to the fool that should release me his own choice of the most cruel form

38

of death by which he should die. Now therefore accept that mercy which I still offer and choose thy penalty!"

When the fisherman heard this he gave himself up for lost, yet he did not the less continue by prayer and supplication to entreat the Genie from his purpose. But when he found that there was no heart left in him to be moved, then for the first time he bestirred his wits, and remembering how that which is evil contains far less wisdom than that which is good, and so falls ever the more readily into the trap prepared for it, he spoke thus: "O Genie, since thou art determined on my death, there is yet a certain thing touching thine honor that I would first know. So, by the Infeffable Name, which is the seal of Solomon, I will ask thee one question, and do thou swear to answer it truly."

The Genie was ready enough to give the oath as desired. Then said the fisherman, "How is it that one so great as thou art, whose feet o'er-step the hills and whose head out-tops the heaven—how can such a one enter into so small a vessel to dwell in it? Truly, though mine eyes tell me I have seen it, I cannot any longer believe so great a marvel."

"What?" cried the Genie, "dost thou not believe what I have already told thee?"

"Not till I have seen it done can I believe it," said the fisherman.

Thereupon, without more waste of words, the Genie, drawing his limbs together and folding himself once more in a thick veil of smoke, descended from his vast altitude into the narrow neck of the brazen vessel till not one shred or film of him remained to view. Then the fisherman with a quick hand replaced the leaden stopper, and laughing, cried to the Genie, "Choose now, thou in thy turn, by what manner of death thou wilt die."

The Genie, hearing himself thus mocked, made violent efforts to escape; but the power of the seal of Solomon held him fast, and the fisherman, ceasing not all the while to revile him for the treachery and baseness which were now to receive their due reward, began to carry the vessel back to the sea's brink. "Now," said he, "thou shalt return to the place whence I drew

thee. And here on the shore I will build myself a hut, and to every fisherman that comes near I will say, 'Look that you fish not in these waters, for herein lies bound a wicked genie that has sworn to put to a cruel death whoever dares to release him.'"

"Nay, nay," cried the Genie, "I did not mean what I said. Ask of me now, and I will give you all the treasures that the world contains, or that your heart can find in it to desire, if only you will set me free!"

The fisherman, being of a mild spirit and with no heart for revenge, sat down to consider what he should do, and all the while the imprisoned Genie continued to appeal to him for compassion with loud promise and lamentation. So, at last, the fisherman, having the fear of God before his eyes, after he had extracted from the Genie a most solemn vow to leave him unharmed, drew out the stopper of lead and released him.

No sooner was he out and restored to his true form than the Genie, turning himself about, lifted his foot and with his full strength smote the brazen vessel far out to sea; and the fisherman, beholding that act, began to repent him of his mercy and to tremble again for dear life.

But the Genie, seeing his fear, broke into huge laughter, and striding on ahead of him cried, "Come, fisherman, and follow me, for now I will lead you to fortune!"

Meekly at his heels went the old fisherman, and leaving behind them the habitations of men they ascended a mountain and entered upon a desert tract guarded by four hills, in the center of which lay a broad lake. Here the Genie stopped, and pointing to a place where fish were swimming in abundance bade the fisherman cast in his net. The fisherman did as he was told, and when he drew in his net he found that it contained four fish each of a different color, a red, a white, a blue, and a yellow: never in his life had he seen the like of them. The Genie bade him take and offer them to the Sultan, assuring him that if he did so they should bring him both fortune and honors. Then he struck the ground with his foot, and immediately the earth opened its mouth and swallowed him as the dry desert swallows the rain.

No sooner had the monarch seen them, so strange of form
and so brilliant and diverse in hue

The fisherman, wondering no less at his safe deliverance than at the marvel of these occurrences, made his way in haste to the city; and there presenting himself at the palace he begged that the four fish might be laid at the Sultan's feet, as a humble offering from the poorest of his subjects.

No sooner had the monarch seen them, so strange of form and so brilliant and diverse in hue, than his longing to taste of them became strongly awakened; so by the hand of his vizier, he sent them to the cook to be prepared forthwith for the royal table. As for the poor fisherman, he received no fewer than four hundred pieces of gold from the Sultan's bounty, and returned to his family rejoicing in an affluence which surpassed his utmost expectations.

The cook meanwhile, proud of an opportunity to exhibit her culinary skill on dainties so rare, scaled and cleaned the fish and laid them in a frying pan over the fire. But scarcely had she done so when the wall of the kitchen divided, and there issued forth from it a damsel of moon-like beauty richly apparelled, holding a rod of myrtle in her hand. With this she struck the fish that lay in the frying pan, and cried:

> "O fish of my pond,
> Are ye true to your bond?"

And immediately the four fish lifted their heads from the frying fat and answered:

> "Even so, the bond holds yet;
> Paid by thee, we pay the debt.
> With give and take is the reckoning met."

Thereupon the damsel upset the pan into the fire and retured through the wall in the same way that she had come, leaving the four fish all charred to a cinder.

The cook, beholding her labor thus brought to naught, began to weep and bewail herself, expecting no less than instant dismissal, and was still loud in her lamentations when the vizier arrived to see if the fish were ready.

On hearing her account of what had occurred, the vizier was greatly astonished, but feared to bring so strange a report to the Sultan's ears while the cravings of the royal appetite were still unsatisfied; so recalling the fisherman by a swift messenger, he bade him procure in all haste four more fish of the same kind, promising to reward him according to the speed with which he accomplished the task. So spurred, and by the additional favor of fortune, the fisherman fulfilled his mission in an astonishingly short space of time; but no sooner was the second lot of fish placed upon the fire in the vizier's presence than once again the wall opened, and the damsel appearing as before, struck the frying pan with her rod, and cried:

"O fish of my pond,
Are ye true to your bond?"

And immediately the fish stood up on their tails in the frying fat and replied:

"Even so, the bond holds yet;
Paid by thee, we pay the debt.
With give and take is the reckoning met."

Whereupon she upset the pan into the fire and departed as she had come.

The vizier, perceiving that so strange an event might no longer be kept from the royal knowledge, went and informed the Sultan of all that had occurred; and the monarch as soon as he had heard the tale, now rendered more eager for the satisfaction of his eyes than he had previously been for the indulgence of his appetite, sent for the fisherman, and promised him yet another four hundred pieces of gold if he could within a given time procure four more fishes similar to those he had already brought on the previous occasions.

If the fisherman had been prompt at the vizier's bidding, he made even greater speed to fulfill the royal command, and before the day was over — this time in the presence of the Sultan himself — four fish, of four diverse colors like to the first, were cleaned and laid into the pan ready for frying. But scarcely had they touched the fat when the wall opened in a clap like thunder,

Recalling the fisherman by a swift messenger

and there came forth with a face of rage a monstrous man the size of a bull, holding in his hand the rod of myrtle. With this he struck the frying pan, and cried in a terrible voice:

> *"O fish from the pond*
> *Are ye true to your bond?"*

And when the fish had returned the same answer that the others had made before them, without more ado the giant overturned the pan upon the fire and departed as he had come.

When the Sultan's eyes had seen that marvel he said to his vizier, "Here is mystery set before us! Surely these fish that talk have a past and a history. Never shall I rest satisfied until I have learned it." So causing the fisherman to be brought before him, he inquired whence the fish came. The fisherman answered, "From a lake between four hills upon the mountain overlooking the city." The Sultan inquired how many days' journey it might be, and the fisherman replied that it was but a matter of a few hours going and returning. Then to the Sultan and his court it seemed that the old man was mocking them, for none had heard tell of any lake lying among the hills so near to that city; and the fisherman, seeing his word doubted, began to fear that the Genie was playing him a trick; for if the lake were now suddenly to vanish, he might find his fortunes more undone at the end than at the beginning.

Yet the Sultan, though his vizier and all his court sought to dissuade him, was firmly resolved on putting the matter to the proof; so he gave orders that an escort and camping tents should be immediately got ready, and with the fisherman to guide, set forth to find the place that was told of.

And, sure enough, when they had ascended the mountain which all knew, they came upon a desert tract on which no man had previously set eyes; and there in its midst lay the lake filled with four kinds of fish, and beyond it stretched a vast and unknown country.

At this sight, so mysterious and unaccountable, of a strange region lying unbeknownst at the gates of his own capital, the monarch was seized with an

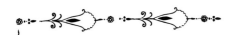

overwhelming desire to press forward in solitary adventure to the discovery of its secret. To the cautious counsels of his vizier he turned a deaf ear; but since it would not be safe for his subjects to know of his departure on an errand so perilous, it was given out that he had been stricken by sudden sickness. The door of the royal tent was closed, and in the dead of night the Sultan, admitting none but the vizier into his confidence, set out secretly on his adventure.

Journeying by night and resting by day, he arrived on the third morning within sight of a palace of shining marble which, with its crowd of domes and minarets, stood solitary among the hills. No sign of life was about it, and when he drew near and knocked at the gates none came to answer him. Then, finding the doors unfastened, he took courage and entered; and advancing through chambers where gold lay as dust, and by fountains wherein pearls lay poured out like water, he found only solitude to greet him.

Wandering without aim among innumerable treasures unguarded and left to waste, the Sultan grew weary, and sat down in an embrasure to rest. Then it seemed to him that not far off he could hear a sorrowful voice chant verses of lamentation. Following the sounds with wonder he came to a curtained doorway, and passing through found himself in the presence of a fair youth richly dressed, seated upon a couch and bearing upon his countenance tokens of extreme grief and despondency. To the Sultan's proffered greeting the youth returned salutation, but did not stir from his seat. "Pardon me," he said, "for not rising; but my miserable condition makes it impossible." Having said this he again broke into doleful lamentation; and when the Sultan inquired as to the cause of so many tears, "See for yourself," he cried, "what I am now made into!" And lifting the skirt of his robe he revealed himself all stone from his waist to the soles of his feet, while from the waist upwards he was as other men. Then as he observed upon his visitor's countenance the expression of a lively curiosity and astonishment, "Doubtless," he went on, "as you now know the secret of my miserable condition you will wish also to hear my story." And he related it as follows:

THE KING OF THE
EBONY ISLES

"My father was King of the city which once stood about this palace. He was lord also of the Ebony Isles that are now the four hills which you passed on your way hither. When I succeeded to the throne upon his death, I took to wife my own cousin, the daughter of my uncle with whom I lived for five years in the utmost confidence and felicity, continually entertained by the charm of her conversation and the beauty of her person, and happy in the persuasion that she found in me an equal satisfaction.

"One day, however, it chanced, in the hour before dinner when the Queen was gone to bathe and adorn herself, that I lay upon a couch beside which two female slaves sat fanning me; and they, supposing me to be asleep, began to talk concerning me and their mistress. 'Ah!' said one, 'how little our lord knows where our mistress goes to amuse herself every night while he lies dreaming!' 'How should he know?' returned the other, 'seeing that the cup of wine which she gives him each night contains a sleeping-draught, that causes him to sleep sound however long she is absent. Then at daybreak when she returns she burns perfumes under his nostrils, and he waking and finding her there guesses nothing. Pity it is that he cannot know of her treacherous ways, for surely it is a shame that a king's wife should go abroad and mix with base people.'

"Now when I heard this the light of day grew dark before my eyes; but I lay on and made no sign, awaiting my wife's return. And she coming in presently, we sat down and ate and drank together according to custom; and afterwards, when I had retired and lain down, she brought me with her own hands the cup of spiced wine, inviting me to drink. Then I, averting myself, raised it to my lips, but instead of drinking, poured it by stealth into my bosom, and immediately sank down as though overcome by its potency, feigning slumber. Straightway the Queen rose up from my side, and having clothed herself in gorgeous apparel and anointed herself with perfumes, she

made her way secretly from the palace, and I with equal secrecy followed her.

"Soon passing by way of the narrower streets, we arived before the city gates; and immediately at a word from her the chains fell and the gates opened of their own accord, closing again behind us as soon as we had passed. At last she came to a ruined hut, and there entering I saw her presently with her veil laid aside, seated in familiar converse with the meanest and most vile of slaves, offering to him in abject servility dainties which she carried from the royal table, and bestowing upon him every imaginable token of affection and regard.

"At this discovery I fell into a blind rage, and drawing my sword I rushed in and struck the slave from behind a blow upon the neck that should have killed him. Then believing that I had verily slain him, and before the Queen found eyes to realize what had befallen, I departed under cover of night as quickly as I had come, and returned to the palace and my own chamber.

"On awaking the next morning I found the Queen lying beside me as though nothing had happened, and at first I was ready to believe it had all been an evil dream; but presently I perceived her eyes red with weeping, her hair dishevelled, and her face torn by the passion of a grief which she strove to conceal. Having thus every reason to believe that my act of vengeance had not fallen short of its purpose, I held my tongue and made no sign.

"But the same day at noon, while I sat in council, the Queen appeared before me clad in deep mourning, and with many tears informed me how she had received sudden news of the death of her father and mother and two brothers, giving full and harrowing details of each event. Without any show of incredulity I heard her tale; and when she besought my permission to go into retirement and mourn in a manner befitting so great a calamity, I bade her do as she desired.

"So for a whole year she continued to mourn in a privacy which I left undisturbed; and during that time she caused to be built a mausoleum or

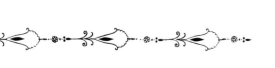

Supposing me asleep, they began to talk

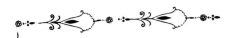 

Temple of Lamentation—the same whose dome you see yonder—into which she withdrew herself from all society; while I, believing the cause of my anger removed and willing to humor the grief which my act had caused her, waited patiently for her return to a sane and reasonable state of mind.

"But, as I learned too late, matters had not so fallen: for though in truth the slave was grievously wounded, being cut through the gullet and speechless, it was not the will of Heaven that he should die; and the Queen having by her enchantments kept him in a sort of life, no sooner was the mausoleum finished than she caused him to be secretly conveyed thither, and there night and day tended him, awaiting his full recovery.

"At length, when two years were over and her mourning in no wise abated, my curiosity became aroused; so going one day to the Temple of Lamentation I entered unannounced, and placing myself where I might see and not be seen, there I discovered her in an abandonment of fond weeping over her miserable treasure whose very life was a dishonor to us both. But no sooner in my just resentment had I started to upbraid her, than she—as now for the first time realizing the cause of her companion's misfortune—began to heap upon me terms of the most violent and shameful abuse; and when, carried beyond myself, I threatened her with my sword, she stood up before me, and having first uttered words of unknown meaning, she cried:

> *'Be thou changed in a moment's span;*
> *Half be marble, and half be man!'*

And at the word I became even as you see me now—dead to the waist, and above living yet bound. Yet even so her vengeance was not satisfied. Having reduced me to this state, she went on to vent her malice upon the city and islands over which I ruled, and the unfortunate people who were my subjects. Thus by her wicked machinations the city became a lake and the islands about it the four hills which you have seen; as for the inhabitants, she turned them into fish of four different colors. And now having done all this she fails not every day to inflict upon me a hundred lashes with a whip which draws

blood at every stroke: and when these are accomplished she covers my torn flesh with hair-cloth and lays over it these rich robes in mockery. Of a surety it is the will of Heaven that I should be the most miserable and despised of mortals!"

Thus the youth finished his story, nor when he had ended could he refrain from tears. The Sultan also was greatly moved when he heard it, and his heart became full of a desire to avenge such injuries upon the doer of them. "Tell me," he said, "where is now the monster of iniquity?" "Sir," answered the youth, "I doubt not she is yonder in the mausoleum with her companion, for thither she goes daily so soon as she has measured out to me my full meed of chastisement: and as for this day my portion has been served to me, I am quit of her till tomorrow brings the hour of fresh scourgings."

Now when this was told him the Sultan saw his way plain. "Be of good cheer," he said to the youth, "and endure with a quiet spirit yet once more the affliction she causes thee; for at the price of that single scourging I trust, by the will of Heaven, to set thee free."

So on the morrow the Sultan lay in close hiding until sounds reached him which told that the whippings had begun; then he arose and went in haste to the mausoleum, where amid rich hangings and perfumes and the illuminations of a thousand candles, he found the slave stretched mute upon a bed, awaiting in great feebleness the recovered use of his sawn gullet. Quickly, with a single sword stroke, the avenger took from him that poor remnant of life which enchantment alone had made possible: then having thrown the body into a well in the courtyard below, he lay down in the dead man's place, drawing the coverlet well over him. Soon after, fresh from her accustomed task of cruelty, the enchantress entered, and falling upon her knees beside the bed she cried, "Has my lord still no voice wherewith to speak to his servant? Surely, for lack of that sound, hearing lies withered within me!" Then the Sultan, taking to himself the speech of the slain man, said, "There is no strength or power but in God alone!"

She went on to vent her malice upon the city and islands

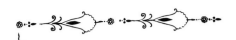

On hearing those words, believing that her companion's speech was at last restored to him, the Queen uttered a cry of joy. But scarcely had she begun to lavish upon him the tokens of her affection when the pretended slave broke out against her in violent abuse. "What!" he cried, "dost thou expect favor at my hands, when it is because of thee that for two years I have lain dumb and prostrate? How darest thou speak to me or look for any recompense save death! Nay!" he went on in answer to her astonished protests, "have not the cries and tears and groans of thy husband kept me continually from rest: and has not Heaven smitten me for no other reason than because thou wouldst not cease from smiting him? So has the curse which thou didst seek to lay upon him fallen doubly upon me."

"Alas!" cried the enchantress, "have I unknowingly caused thee so great an ill? If it be so, then let my lord give command, and whatever be his desire it shall be satisfied."

Then said the Sultan, "Go instantly and release thy husband from spell and torment: and when it is done, return hither with all speed."

Thus compelled, in great fear and bewilderment and sorely against her will, the Queen sped to the chamber in the palace where her husband lay spellbound. Taking a vessel of water she pronounced over it certain words which caused it instantly to boil as though it had been set on a fire: then throwing the water over him, she cried:

"Spell be loosed, and stone grow warm,
Yield back flesh to the human form."

And immediately on the word his nature came to him again, and he leaped and stood upon his feet. But the Queen's hatred towards him was by no means abated. "Go hence quickly," she cried, "since a better will than mine releases thee! But if thou tarry or if thou return thou shalt surely die!" Thankful for his deliverance the youth stayed not to question, but departing went and hid himself without, while the Queen returned in haste to the mausoleum where her supposed lover awaited her. There, eager for restora-

tion to favor, she informed him of what she had done, supposing that to be all.

"Nay," said the other, still speaking with the voice of the slave; "though thou hast lopped the branch of evil thou hast not destroyed the root. For every night I hear a jumping of fish in the lake that is between the four hills, and the sound of their curses on thee and me comes to disturb my rest. Go instantly and restore all things to their former state, then come back and give me thy hand and I shall rise up a sound man once more."

Rejoicing in that promise and the expectations it held out to her of future happiness, the Queen went with all speed to the border of the lake. There taking a little water into her hand, and uttering strange words over it, she sprinkled it this way and that upon the surface of the lake and the roots of the four hills, and immediately where had been the lake a city appeared, and instead of fishes inhabitants, and in place of the four hills four islands. As for the palace, it stood no longer removed far away into the desert but upon a hill overlooking the city.

Great was the astonishment of the vizier and the Sultan's escort which had lain encamped beside the lake to find themselves suddenly transported to the heart of a populous city, with streets and walls and the hum of reawakened life around them; but a greater and more terrible shock than this awaited the Queen upon her return to the mausoleum to enjoy the reward of her labors. "Now," she cried, "let my lord arise, since all that he willed is accomplished!"

"Give me thy hand!" said the Sultan, still in a voice of disguise; "come nearer that I may lean on thee!" And as she approached he drew forth his sword which had lain concealed beside him in the bed, and with a single blow cleft her wicked body in twain.

Then he rose and went quickly to where in hiding lay the young King her husband, who learned with joy of the death of his cruel enemy. He thanked the Sultan with tears of gratitude for his deliverance, and invoked the blessings of Heaven upon him and his kingdom. "On yours too," said the Sultan,

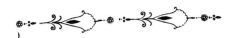 

"let peace and prosperity now reign! And since your city is so near to mine, come with me and be my guest that we may rejoice together in the bonds of friendship."

"Nay," answered the young King, "that would I do willingly, but your country lies many a day's journey from my own. I fear the breaking of the spell which held me and my subjects has brought you farther than you wished."

It was in fact true that the Ebony Isles had now returned to the place from which they had originally come. The Sultan put a smiling face upon the matter: "I can well put up with the tedium of my journey," said he, "if only you will be my companion. Nay, let me speak frankly to one whose demeanor in affliction has won my heart; I am childless and have no heir. Come with me and be my son, and when I am dead unite our two kingdoms under a single ruler." The young King, who had conceived for his deliverer an equal affection, could not withstand so noble and generous an offer; and so with a free exchange of hearts on both sides the matter was arranged.

After a journey of some months the Sultan arrived again at his own capital, where he was welcomed with great rejoicings by the people, who had long mourned over his strange and unexplained absence.

As for the old fisherman who had been the immediate cause of the young King's deliverance, the Sultan loaded him with honors and gave his daughters in marriage to sons of the blood royal, so that they all continued in perfect happiness and contentment to the end of their days.

THE MAGIC HORSE

*At so arrogant a claim all the courtiers
burst into loud laughter*

IN the land of the Persians there lived in ancient times a King who had three daughters and an only son of such beauty that they drew the eyes of all beholders like moonrise in a clear heaven. Now it was the custom in that country for a great festival to be held at the new year, during which people of all grades, from the highest to the lowest, presented themselves before the King with offerings and salutations. So it happened that on one of these days there came to the King as he sat in state three sages, masters of their craft, bringing gifts for approval. The first had with him a peacock of gold which was so constructed that at the passing of each hour it beat its wings and uttered a cry. And the King, having proved it, found the gift acceptable and caused the inventor thereof to be suitably rewarded. The second had made a trumpet so that if placed over the gates of a city it blew a blast against any that sought to enter; and thus was the city held safe from surprise by an enemy. And when the King had found that it possessed that property, he accepted it, bestowing on its maker a rich reward.

But the gift of the third sage, who was an Indian, appeared more prodigious than all, for he had brought with him a horse of ivory and ebony, for which he claimed that, at the will of its owner, or of anyone instructed in the secret, it would rise above the earth and fly, arriving at distant places in a marvellously short space of time. The King, full of wonder at such a statement, and eager to test it, was in some doubt as to how he might do so, for the Indian was unwilling to part with the secret until secure of the reward which in his own mind he had fixed on. Now it happened that at a distance of some three leagues from the city there stood a mountain the top of which was clearly discernible to all eyes; so, in order that the Indian's word might be proved, the King, pointing to it, said, "Go yonder, and bring back to me while I wait the branch of a palm tree which grows at the foot of that mountain; then I shall know that what you tell me is true."

Instantly the Indian set foot in the stirrup and vaulted upon his charger, and scarcely had he turned a small peg which was set in the pommel of the saddle, when the horse rose lightly into the air and bore him away at wondrous speed amid the shouts of the beholders; and while all were still gazing, amazed at so sudden a vanishing, he reappeared high overhead, bearing the palm branch, and descending into their midst alighted upon the very spot from which he had started, where, prostrating himself, he laid the branch at the King's feet.

The King was so delighted when the wonderful properties of the horse had been thus revealed to him, that, eager to possess it, he bade the Indian name his own reward, declaring that no price could be too great. Then said the sage, "Since your Majesty so truly appreciates the value of my invention, I do not fear that the reward I ask for will seem too high. Give me in marriage the hand of the fairest of your three daughters, and the horse shall be yours."

At so arrogant a claim all the courtiers burst into loud laughter; the King alone, consumed with the desire of possessing the wonderful treasure, hesitated as to what answer he should give. Then the King's son, Prince Firouz Schah, seeing his father lend ear to so shameful a proposal, became moved with indignation. Determined to defend his sister's honor and his own, he addressed the King. "Pardon me, sire," said he, "if I take the liberty of speaking. But how shall it be possible for one of the greatest and most powerful monarchs to ally himself to a mere nobody? I entreat you to consider what is due not to yourself alone but to the high blood of your ancestors and of your children."

"My son," replied the King of Persia, "what you say is very true, so far as it goes; but you do not sufficiently consider the value of so incomparable a marvel as this horse has proved itself to be, or how great would be my chagrin if any other monarch came to possess it. And though I have not yet agreed to the Indian's proposal, I cannot incontinently reject it. But first I

must be satisfied that the horse will obey other hands besides those of its inventor, else, though I become its possessor, I may find it useless."

The Indian, who had stood aside during this discussion, was now full of hope, for he perceived that the King had not altogether rejected his terms, and nothing seemed likelier than that the more he became familiar with the properties of the magic horse the more would he wish to possess it. When, therefore, the King proposed that the horse should be put to a more independent trial under another rider, the Indian readily agreed; the more so when the Prince himself, relinquishing his apparent opposition, came forward and volunteered for the essay.

The King having consented, the Prince mounted, and eager in his design to give his father opportunity for cooler reflection, he did not wait to hear all the Indian's instructions, but turning the peg, as he had seen the other do when first mounting, caused the horse to rise suddenly in the air, and was carried away out of sight in an easterly direction more swiftly than an arrow shot from a bow.

No sooner had the horse and its rider disappeared than the King became greatly concerned for his son's safety; and though the sage could justly excuse himself on the ground that the young Prince's impatience had caused him to cut short the instructions which would have ensured his safe return, the King chose to vent upon the Indian the full weight of his displeasure; and cursing the day wherein he had first set eyes on the magic horse, he caused its maker to be thrown into prison, declaring that if the Prince did not return within a stated time the life of the other should be forfeit.

The Indian had now good cause to repent of the ambition which had brought him to this extremity, for the Prince, of whose opposition to his project he had been thoroughly informed, had only to prolong his absence to involve him in irretrievable ruin. But on the failure of arrogant pretensions the sympathy of the judicious is wasted; let us return therefore to Prince Firouz Schah, whom we left flying through the air with incredible swiftness on the back of the magic steed.

For a time, confident of his skill as a rider and undismayed either by the speed or altitude of his flight, the Prince had no wish to return to the palace; but presently the thought of his father's anxiety occurred to him, and being of a tender and considerate disposition he immediately endeavoured to divert his steed from its forward course. This he sought to do by turning in the contrary direction the peg which he had handled when mounting, but to his astonishment the horse responded by rising still higher in the air and flying forward with redoubled swiftness. Had courage then deserted him, his situation might have become perilous; but preserving his accustomed coolness he began carefully to search for the means by which the speed of the machine might be abated, and before long he perceived under the horse's mane a smaller peg, which he had no sooner touched than he felt himself descending rapidly toward the earth, with a speed that lessened the nearer he came to ground.

As he descended, the daylight in which hitherto he had been travelling faded from view, and he passed within a few minutes from sunset into an obscurity so dense that he could no longer distinguish the nature of his environment, till, as the horse alighted, he perceived beneath him a smooth expanse ending abruptly on all sides at an apparent elevation among the objects surrounding it.

Dismounting he found himself on the roof of a large palace, with marble balustrades dividing it in terraces, and at one side a staircase which led down to the interior. With a spirit ever ready for adventure Prince Firouz Schah immediately descended, groping his way through the darkness till he came to a landing on the farther side of which an open door led into a room where a dim light was burning.

The Prince paused at the doorway to listen, but all he could hear was the sound of men breathing heavily in their sleep. He pushed the door and entered; and there across an inner threshold he saw black slaves lying asleep,

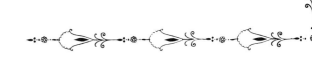

each with a drawn sword in his hand. Immediately he guessed that something far more fair must lie beyond; so, undeterred by the danger, he advanced, and stepping lightly across their swords passed through silken hangings into the inner chamber. Here he perceived, amid surroundings of regal magnificence, a number of couches, one of which stood higher than the rest. Upon each of these a fair damsel lay asleep; but upon that which was raised above its fellows lay a form of such perfect and enchanting beauty that the Prince had no will or power to turn away after once beholding it. Approaching the sleeper softly, he kneeled down and plucked her gently by the sleeve; and immediately the Princess—for such if rank and beauty accorded she must be—opened to him the depths of her lustrous eyes and gazed in quiet amazement at the princely youth whose handsome looks and reverent demeanor banished at once all thought of alarm.

Now it so happened that a son of the King of India was at that time seeking the hand of the Princess in marriage; but her father, the King of Bengal, had rejected him owing to his ferocious and disagreeable aspect. When therefore the Princess saw one of royal appearance kneeling before her she supposed he could be no other than the suitor who she knew only by report, and shedding upon him the light of her regard, "By Allah," she said, smiling, "my father lied in saying that good looks were lacking to thee!"

Prince Firouz Schah, perceiving from these words and the glance which accompanied them, that her disposition towards him was favorable, no longer feared to acquaint her with the plight in which he found himself; while the Princess, for her part, listened to the story of his adventures with lively interest, and learned, not without secret satisfaction, that her visitor possessed a rank and dignity equal to her own.

Meanwhile the maidens who were in attendance on the Princess had awakened in dismay to the unaccountable apparition of a fair youth kneeling at the feet of their mistress, and, dreading discovery by the attendants, were

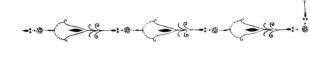

all at a loss what to do. The Princess, however, seeing that they were awake, called them to her with perfect composure and bade them go instantly and prepare an inner chamber where the Prince might sleep and recover from the fatigues of his journey; at the same time she gave orders for a rich banquet to be prepared for the time when he should be ready to partake of it. Then when her visitor had retired, she arose and began to adorn herself in jewels and rich robes and to anoint her body with fragrance, giving her women no rest till the tale of her mirror contented her; and when all had been done many times over, and the last touch of art added to her loveliness, she sent to inquire whether the Prince had yet awaked and was ready to receive her.

Upon the receipt of that message the Prince rose eagerly, and dressing in haste, although it was scarcely yet day, heard everywhere within the palace sounds of preparation for the feast that was being got ready in his honor.

Before long the Princess herself entered to inquire how he had slept, and being fully assured on that score, she gave orders for the banquet to be served. Everything was done in the greatest magnificence, but the Princess was full of apologies, declaring the entertainment unworthy of so distinguished a guest. "You must pardon me, Prince," she said, "for receiving you with so little state, and after so hasty a preparation; but the chief of the eunuchs does not enter here without my express permission, and I feared that elsewhere our conversation might be interrupted."

Prince Firouz Schah was now convinced that the inclinations of the Princess corresponded with his own; but though her every word and movement increased the tenderness of his passion, he did not forget the respect due to her rank and virtue. One of her women attendants, however, seeing clearly in what direction matters were tending, and fearing for herself the results of a sudden discovery, withdrew secretly, saying nothing to the rest, and running quickly to the chief of the guards she cried, "O miserable man, what sorry watch is this that thou hast kept, guarding the King's honor;

and who is this man or genie that thou hast admitted to the presence of our mistress? Nay, if the matter be not already past remedy the fault is not thine!"

At these words he quickly leapt up in alarm, and going secretly he lifted the curtain of the inner chamber, and there beheld at the Princess's side a youth of such fair and majestical appearance that he durst not intrude unbidden. He ran shrieking to the King, and as he went he rent his garments and threw dust upon his head. "O sire and master," he cried, "come quickly and save thy daughter, for there is with her a genie in mortal form and like a king's son to look upon, and if he has not already carried her away, make haste and give orders that he be seized, lest thou become childless."

The King at once arose and went in great haste and fear to his daughter's palace. There he was met by certain of her women, who, seeing his alarm, said, "O sire, have no fear for the safety of thy daughter; for this young man is as handsome of heart as of person, and as his conduct is chaste, so also are his intentions honorable."

Then the King's wrath was cooled somewhat; but since much remained which demanded explanation he drew his sword and advanced with a threatening aspect into the room where his daughter and the Prince still sat conversing. Prince Firouz Schah, observing the newcomer advance upon him in a warlike attitude, drew his sword and stood ready for defense; whereupon the King, seeing that the other was the stronger, sheathed his weapon, and with a gesture of salutation addressed him courteously. "Tell me, fair youth," he said, "whether you are man or devil, for though in appearance you are human, how else than by devilry have you come here?"

"Sire," replied the youth, "but for the respect that is owing to the father of so fair a daughter, I, who am a son of kings, might resent such an imputation. Be assured, however, that by whatever means I have chosen to arrive, my intentions now are altogether human and honorable; for I have no other or dearer wish than to become your son-in-law through my marriage with this Princess in whose eyes it is my happiness to have found favor."

"What you tell me," answered the King, "may be all very true; but it is not the custom for the sons of kings to enter into palaces without the permission of their owners, coming, moreover, unannounced and with no retinue or mark of royalty about them. How, then, shall I convince my people that you are a fit suitor for the hand of my daughter?"

"The proof of honor and kingship," answered the other, "does not rest in splendor and retinue alone, though these also would be at my call had I the patience to await their arrival from that too distant country where my father is King. Let it suffice if I shall be able to prove my worth alone and unaided, in such a manner as to satisfy all." "Alone and unaided?" said the King; "how may that be?" "I will prove it thus," answered the Prince. "Call out your troops and let them surround this palace; tell them that you have here a stranger, of whom nothing is known, who declares that if you will not yield him the hand of your daughter in marriage he will carry her away from you by force. Bid them use all means to capture and slay me, and if I survive so unequal a contest, judge then whether or no I am fit to become your son-in-law."

The King immediately accepted the proposal, agreeing to abide by the result; yet was he grieved that a youth of such fair looks and promise should throw away his life in so foolhardy an adventure. As soon as day dawned he sent for his vizier and bade him cause all the chiefs of his army to assemble with their troops and companies, till presently there were gathered about the palace forty thousand horsemen and the same number of footmen; and the King gave them instructions, saying, "When the young man of whom I have warned you comes forth and challenges you to battle, then fall upon and slay him, for in no wise must he escape." He then led the Prince to an open space whence he could see the whole army drawn up in array against him. "Yonder," said the King, pointing, "are those with whom you have to contend; go forth and deal with them as seems best to you."

"Nay," answered the Prince, "these are not fair conditions, for yonder I see horsemen as well as footmen; how shall I contend against these unless I be mounted?" The King at once offered him the best horse in his stables, but the Prince would not hear of it. "Is it fair," he said, "that I should trust my life under such conditions to a horse that I have never ridden? I will ride no horse but that upon which I came hither."

"Where is that?" inquired the King. "If it be where I left it," answered the Prince, "it is upon the roof of the palace."

All who heard this answer were filled with laughter and astonishment, for it seemed impossible that a horse could have climbed to so high a roof. Nevertheless the King commanded that search should be made, and there, sure enough, those that were sent found the horse of ebony and ivory standing stiff and motionless. So though it still seemed to them but a thing for jest and mockery obeying the King's orders they raised it upon their shoulders, and bearing it to earth carried it forth into the open space before the palace where the King's troops were assembled.

Then Prince Firouz Schah advanced, and leaping upon the horse he cried defiance to the eighty thousand men that stood in battle array against him. And they, on their part, seeing the youth so hardily set on his own destruction, drew sword and couched spear, and came all together to the charge. The Prince waited till they were almost upon him, then turning the peg which stood in the pommel of his saddle he caused the horse to rise suddenly in the air, and all the foremost ranks of the enemy came clashing together beneath him. At that sight the King and all his court drew a breath of astonishment, and the army staggered and swung about this way and that, striking vainly up at the hoofs of the magic horse as it flew over them. Then the King, full of dread lest this should indeed be some evil genie that sought to carry his daughter away from him, called to his archers to shoot, but before they could make ready their bows Prince Firouz Schah had given another turn to the

peg, and immediately the horse sprang upward and rose higher than the roof of the palace, so that all the arrows fell short and rained destruction on those that were below.

Then the Prince called to the King, "O King of Bengal, have I not now proved myself worthy to be thy son-in-law, and wilt thou not give me the hand of thy daughter in marriage?" But the King's wrath was very great, for he had been made foolish in the eyes of his people, and panic had broken the ranks of his army and many of them were slain; and by no means would he have for his son-in-law one that possessed such power to throw down the order and establishment of his kingdom. So he cried back to the Prince, saying, "O vile enchanter, get hence as thou valuest thy life, for if ever thou darest to return and set foot within my dominions thy death and not my daughter shall be thy reward!" Thus he spoke in his anger, forgetting altogether the promise he had made.

Now it should be known that all this time the Princess had been watching the combat from the roof of the palace; and as her fear and anxiety for the Prince had in the first instance been great, so now was she overjoyed when she saw him rise superior to the dangers which had threatened him. But as soon as she heard her father's words she became filled with fresh fear lest she and her lover were now to be parted; so as the Prince came speeding by upon the magic horse she stretched up her arms to him, crying, "O master of the flying bird, leave me not desolate, for if thou goest from me now I shall die."

No sooner did Prince Firouz Schah hear those words than he checked his steed in its flight, and swooping low he bore down over the palace roof, and catching the Princess up in his arms placed her upon the saddle before him; and straightway at the pressure of its rider the horse rose under them and carried them away high in the air, so that they disappeared forthwith from the eyes of the King and his people.

But as they travelled the day grew hot and the sun burned fiercely upon them; and the Prince looking down beheld a green meadow by the side of a lake: so he said, "O desire of my heart, let us go down into yonder meadow and seek rest and refreshment, and there let us wait till it is evening, so that we may come unperceived to my father's palace, and when I have brought thee thither safely and secretly, then will I make preparation so that thou mayest appear at my father's court in such a manner as befits thy rank."

So the Princess consenting, they went down and sat by the lake and solaced themselves sweetly with love till it was evening. Then they rose up and mounted once more upon the magic horse and came by night to the outskirts of the city where dwelt the King of Persia. Now in the garden of the summer palace which stood without the walls all was silence and solitude, and coming thither unnoticed the King's son led the Princess to a pavilion, the door of which lay open, and placing before it the magic horse he bade her stay within and keep watch till his messenger should come to take her to the palace which he would cause to be prepared for her.

Leaving her thus safely sheltered, the Prince went into the city to present himself before the King his father; and there he found him in deep mourning and affliction because of his son's absence; and his father seeing him, rose up and embraced him tenderly, rejoicing because of his safe return, and eager to know in what way he had fared. And the Prince said, "O my father, if it be thy good will and pleasure, I have come back to thee far richer than I went. For I have brought with me the fairest Princess that the eyes of love have ever looked upon, and she is the daughter of the King of Bengal; and because of my love for her and the great service which she rendered me when I was a stranger in the midst of enemies, therefore have I no heart or mind or will but to win your consent that I may marry her." And when the King heard that, and of all that the Princess had done, and of how they had escaped together, he gave his consent willingly, and ordered that a palace should be

immediately got ready for her reception that she might on the next day appear before the people in a manner befitting her rank.

Then while preparation was going forward, the Prince sought news concerning the sage, for he feared that the King might have slain him. "Do not speak of him," cried the King. "Would to Heaven that I had never set eyes on him or his invention, for out of this has arisen all my grief and lamentation. Therefore he now lies in prison awaiting death."

"Nay," said the Prince, "now surely should he be released and suitably rewarded, seeing that unwittingly he hath been the cause of my fortune; but do not give him my sister in marriage."

So the King sent and caused the Indian to be brought before him clad in a robe of rank. And the King said to him, "Because my son, whom thy vile invention carried away from me, hath returned safe and sound, therefore will I spare thy life. And for the reward of thine ingenuity I give thee this robe of honor; but now take thy horse, whatever it may be, and go, nor ever appear in my sight again. And if thou wilt marry, seek one of thine own rank, but do not aspire to the daughters of kings."

When the Indian heard that, he dissembled his rage, and bowing himself to the earth departed from the King's presence. And, as he went, everywhere in the palace ran the tale how the King's son had returned upon the magic horse bringing with him a Princess of most marvellous beauty, and how they had alighted in the gardens of the summer palace that lay outside the walls.

Now when this was told him the Indian at once saw his opportunity, and going forth from the city in haste he arrived at the summer palace before the messenger with the appointed retinue which the Prince and the King were sending. So coming to the pavilion in the garden he found the Princess waiting within, and before the door the horse of ivory and ebony. Then was his heart uplifted for joy, the more so when he perceived how far the damsel exceeded in loveliness all that had been told of her. Entering the chamber

where she sat he kissed the ground at her feet; and she, seeing one that wore a robe of office making obeisance before her, spake to him without fear, saying, "Who art thou?"

The sage answered, "O moon of beauty, I am but the dust which lies upon the road by which thou art to travel. Yet I come as a messenger from the King's son who hath sent me to bring thee with all speed to a chamber in the royal palace where he now awaits thee."

Now the Indian was of a form altogether hideous and abominable. The Princess looked at him, therefore, in surprise, saying, "Could not the King's son find anyone to send to me but thee?" The sage laughed, for he read the meaning of her words. "O searcher of hearts," he said, "do not wonder that the Prince hath sent to thee a man whose looks are unattractive, for because of his love toward thee he is grown exceedingly jealous. Were it otherwise, I doubt not that he would have chosen the highest and most honorable in the land; but, being what I am, he has preferred to make me his messenger."

When the Princess heard that, she believed him, and because her impatience to be with her lover was great, she yielded herself willingly into his hands. Then the sage mounted upon the horse and took up the damsel behind him; and having bound her to his girdle for safety, he turned the pin so swiftly that immediately they rose up into the air far above the roof of the palace and in full view of the royal retinue which was even then approaching.

Now because his desire to be with his beloved was so strong, the Prince himself had come forth before all others to meet her; and when he saw her thus carried away captive, he uttered a loud cry of lamentation, and stretched out his hands toward her. The cry of her lover reached the ears of the Princess, and looking down she saw with wonder his gestures of grief and despair. So she said to the Indian, "O slave, why art thou bearing me away from thy lord, disobeying his command?" The sage answered, "He is not my lord, nor do I owe him any duty or obedience. May Heaven repay on him all the grief he has brought on me, for I was the maker of this horse on which he

won thee, and because he stole it from me I was cast into prison. But now for all my wrongs I will take full payment, and will torture his heart as he hath tortured mine. Be of good cheer, therefore, for doubt not that presently I shall seem a more desirable lover in thine eyes than ever he was."

On hearing these words the Princess was so filled with terror and loathing that she endeavored to cast herself from the saddle; but the Indian having bound her to his girdle, no present escape from him was possible.

The horse had meanwhile carried them far from the city of the King of Persia, and it was yet an early hour after dawn when they arrived over the land of Cashmere. Assured that he was now safe from pursuit, and perceiving an uninhabited country below him, the Indian caused the horse to descend on the edge of a wood bordered by a stream. Here he made the Princess dismount, and was proceeding to force upon her his base and familiar attentions, when the cries raised by the Princess drew to that spot a party of horsemen who had been hunting in the neighborhood. The leader of the party, who chanced to be no other than the Sultan of that country, seeing a fair damsel undergoing ill-treatment from one of brutish and malevolent appearance, rode forward and demanded of the Indian by what right he so used her. The sage boldly declared that she was his wife and that how he treated her was no man's business but his own. The damsel, however, contradicted his assertion with indignation and scorn, and so great were her beauty and the dignity of her bearing that her statement of the case had only to be heard to be believed. The Sultan therefore ordered the Indian to be led away to the adjacent city and there cast into the deepest dungeon. As for the Princess and magic horse, he caused them to be brought to the palace, and there for the damsel he provided a magnificent apartment with slaves and attendants such as befitted her rank; but the horse, whose properties remained secret, since no other use for it could be discovered, was placed in the royal treasury.

Now though the Princess was full of joy over her escape from the Indian, and of gratitude to her deliverer, she could not fail to read in the Sultan's

manner towards her the spell cast by her beauty. And, in fact, no later than the next day, awakened by sounds of tumult and rejoicing throughout the city, and inquiring as to the reason, she was informed that these festivities were the prelude to her own wedding with the Sultan which was to be celebrated that very day before sundown.

At this news her consternation was so great that she immediately swooned away, and remained for a long while speechless. But no sooner had she recovered possession of her faculties than her resolution was formed, and when the Sultan entered, as is customary on such occasions, to present his compliments and make inquiries as to her health, she fell into an extravagance of attitude and speech, so artfully contrived that all who beheld her became convinced of her insanity. And the more surely to effect her purpose, and at the same time to relieve her feelings, she made a violent attack upon the Sultan's person; nor did she desist until she had brought him to recognize that all hopes for the present consummation of the marriage were useless.

On the following day also, and upon every succeeding one, the Princess showed the same violent symptoms whenever the Sultan approached her. It was in vain that all the wisest physicians in the country were summoned into consultation. While some declared that her malady was curable, others, to whose word the Princess by her actions lent every possible weight, declared that it was incurable; and in no case was any remedy applied that did not seem immediately to aggravate the disorder.

And here for a while we must leave the Princess and return to Prince Firouz Schah, whose affliction no words can describe. Unable to endure the burden of his beloved one's absence in the splendors of his father's palace, or to leave her the victim of fate without an attempt at rescue, he put on the disguise of a travelling dervish, and departing secretly from the Persian court set out into the world to seek for her.

For many months he travelled without clue or tidings to guide him; but as Heaven ever bestows favor on constancy in love, so it led him at last to the

land of Cashmere, and to the city of its Sultan. Now as he drew near to it by the main road, he fell into conversation with a certain merchant, and inquired of him as to the city and the life and conditions of its inhabitants. And the merchant looked at him in surprise, saying, "Surely you have come from a far country not to have heard of the strange things which have happened here, for everywhere in these regions and among all the caravans goes the story of the strange maiden, and the ebony horse, and the waiting marriage."

Now when the Prince heard that, he knew that the end of his wanderings was in sight: so looking upon the city with eyes of gladness, "Tell me," he said, "for I know none of these things." So the merchant told him truly all that has here been narrated; and having ended he said, "O dervish, though you are young, you have in your eyes the light of wisdom; and if you have also in your hands the power of healing, then I tell you that in this city fortune awaits you, for the Sultan will give even the half of his kingdom to any man that shall restore health of mind to this damsel."

Then the King's son felt his heart uplifted within him, although he knew well that the fortune he sought would not be of the Sultan's choosing; so parting from the merchant, he put on the robe of a physician, and went and presented himself at the palace.

The Sultan was glad at his coming, for though many physicians had promised healing and had all failed, still each new arrival gave him fresh hopes. Now as the sight of a physician seemed ever greatly to increase the Princess's malady, the Sultan led him to a small closet or balcony, that thence he might look upon her unseen. So Prince Firouz Schah, having travelled so many miles in search of her, saw his beloved seated in deep despondency by the side of a fountain; and ever with the tears falling down from her eyes she sighed and sang. Now when he heard her voice and the words, and beheld the soft grief of her countenance, then the Prince knew that her disorder was only feigned; and he went forth and said to the Sultan, "This malady is curable; but for the cure something is yet lacking. Let me go in and speak with the

Till the tale of her mirror contented her

damsel alone, and on my life I promise that if all be done according to my requirements, before this time tomorrow the cure shall be accomplished."

At these words the Sultan rejoiced greatly, and he ordered the doors of the Princess's chamber to be opened to the physician. So Firouz Schah passed in, and he and his beloved were alone together. Now because of his grief and wanderings and the growth of his beard, the face of the Prince was so changed that the Princess did not know him; but seeing one before her in the dress of a physician she rose up in pretended frenzy and began to throw herself about with violence, until from utter exhaustion she fell prostrate. Thereupon the Prince drew near, and called her gently by name; and immediately when she heard his voice she knew him, and uttered a loud cry. Then the King's son put his mouth to her ear and said, "O temptation of all hearts, now spare my life and have patience, for surely I am come to save thee; but if the Sultan learn who I am we are dead, thou and I, because his jealousy is great." So she replied, saying, "O thou that bringest me life, tell me what I shall do?" The Prince said, "When I depart hence let it appear that I have restored to thee the possession of thy faculties; although the full cure is to come after. Therefore when the Sultan comes to thee, be sad and meek and do not repulse him as thou hast done before. Yet have no fear but that I will keep thee safe from him to the last." And so saying he left the Princess and returned to the Sultan, and said to him, "Go in and see whether the cure be not already at work; but approach not near to her, for though the genie that possessed her is bound he is not yet cast forth: nevertheless tomorrow before noon the remedy shall be complete."

So the Sultan went and found her even as he had been told; and with joy and gratitude he returned to Firouz Schah, saying, "'Truly thou art a healer and the rest are but bunglers and fools. Now, therefore, give orders and all shall be done according to thy will. Doubt not that thy reward shall be great."

Then the Prince said, "Let the horse of ivory and ebony which was with her at the first be brought forth and set again in the place where it was found,

and let the damsel also be brought and put into my hand; and it shall be that when I have set her upon the horse, then the evil genie that held her shall be suddenly loosed, passing from her into that which was before his place of bondage. So shall the remedy be complete, and the Princess find joy in her lord before the eyes of all."

Now when the Sultan heard that, the mystery of the ebony horse seemed plain to him, and its use manifest. Therefore he gave orders that with all speed the thing should be done as the physician of the Princess required it.

So early on the morrow they brought the horse from the royal treasury, and the Princess from her chamber, and carried them to the place where they were first found; and all about, a great crowd of the populace was gathered to behold the sight. Then Prince Firouz Schah took the Princess and set her upon the horse, and leaping into the saddle before her he turned the pin of ascent, and immediately the horse rose with a great sound into the air, and hung above the heads of the frightened populace. And the King's son leaned down from the saddle and cried in a loud voice, "O Sultan of Cashmere, when you wish to espouse Princesses which seek your protection, learn first to obtain their consent." And so saying he put the horse to its topmost speed, and like an arrow on the wind he and the Princess were borne away, and vanished, and were no more seen in that land.

But in the city of the King of Persia great joy and welcome and thanksgiving awaited them; and there without delay the wedding occurred, and through all the country the people rejoiced and feasted for a full month. But because of the grief and affliction that it had caused him the King broke the ebony horse and destroyed its motions. Thus is the story of the sage and his invention brought to a full ending.

THE WICKED
HALF-BROTHERS

IN the city of Harran there once lived a King who had every happiness which life and fortune could bestow save that he lacked an heir. Although, according to royal custom, he had in his household fifty wives, fair to look upon and affectionate in disposition, and though he continually invoked on these unions the blessing of Heaven, still he remained childless; for which cause all his joy was turned to affliction, and his wealth and power and magnificence became as of no account.

Now one night as he slept there appeared before him an old man of venerable appearance who, addressing him in mild accents, spoke thus: "The prayer of the faithful among fifty has been heard. Arise, therefore, and go into the gardens of your palace and cause the gardener to bring you a pomegranate fully ripe. Eat as many of the seeds as you desire children, and your wish shall be fulfilled."

Immediately upon awaking the King remembered the dream, and going down into the gardens of the palace he took fifty pomegranate seeds, and counting them one by one ate them all. So in due course, according to the promise of his dream, each of his wives gave birth to a son, all about the same time. To this, however, there was an exception, for one of the fifty whose name was Pirouzè, the fairest and the most honorably born, she alone, as time went on, showed no sign of that which was expected of her. Then was the King's anger kindled against her because in her alone the promise of his dream was not fulfilled; and deeming such a one hateful in the eyes of Heaven he was minded to put her to death. His vizier, however, dissuaded him. "Time alone can show," said he, "whether her demerits are so great as you now suppose. Let her go back to her own people, and remain in banishment until the will of Heaven shall declare itself, and if within due time she gives birth to a son then can she return to you with all honor." So the King did as his vizier advised, and sent Pirouzè back to her own country to the court of

the Prince of Samaria; and there before long she who had seemd barren had the joy of becoming a mother and gave birth to a son whom she named Codadad, that is to say, "the Gift of God." Nevertheless, because the King of Harran had put upon her so public a disgrace, the Prince of Samaria would send no word to him of the event; so the young Prince was brought up at his uncle's court, and there he learned to ride and to shoot and to perform such warlike feats as became a prince, and in all that country he had no equal for accomplishment or courage.

One day, when Codadad had reached the age of eighteen, word came to him that his father, the King of Harran, was engaged in war and surrounded by enemies; so the Prince said to his mother, "Now it is time that I should go and prove myself worthy of my birth and the equal of my brethren; for here in Samaria all is peace and indolence, but in Harran are hardship and dangers, and great deeds waiting to be done." And his mother said to him, "O my son, since it seems good to thee, go; but how wilt thou declare thyself to thy father, or cause him to believe thy word, seeing that he is ignorant of thy birth?" Codadad answered, "I will so declare myself by my deeds that before my father knows the truth he shall wish that it were true."

So he departed and came in princely arms to the city of Harran, and there offered his service to the King against all his enemies. Now, no sooner had the King looked upon the youth than his heart was drawn toward him because of his beauty and the secret ties of blood, but when he asked from what country he came, Codadad answered, "I am the son of an emir of Cairo, and wherever there is war I go to win fame, nor do I care in what cause I fight so long as I be proved worthy."

The Prince was not slow in making his valour known; before long he had risen to the command of the whole army, not only over the heads of his brethren but also of the more experienced officers. And thereafter, when peace was reestablished, the King, finding Codadad as prudent as he was valiant, appointed him governor to the young Princes.

Pirouzè, the fairest and most honorably born

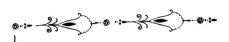

Now this act, though justified by merit, could not fail to increase the hatred and jealousy which Codadad's brethren had long felt towards him. "What?" they cried, "shall this stranger not only steal from us the first place in the King's favor, but must we also be in obedience to his ruling and judgment? Surely if we do so we are no sons of a King."

So they conspired together how best to be rid of him. One said, "Let us fall upon him with our swords." "No, no," said another, "for so doing we shall but bring punishment upon ourselves. But let us so arrange matters as to draw on him the weight of the King's anger; thus shall our vengeance be made both safe and complete."

To this the other Princes agreed; so forming a plan which seemed favorable to their end they approached Codadad, and besought his permission to go forth together on a hunting expedition, promising to return the same day. Codadad, deeming the request reasonable, immediately granted it: the brothers departed, but they did not return.

On the third day the King made inquiry as to the reason of their absence. Codadad replied that they had gone on a hunting expedition but had promised to return much sooner. Another day passed and the King grew anxious; yet another, and he became furious; and all his wrath was directed against Codadad. "O traitor," he cried, "why hast thou neglected thy trust and allowed my sons to go anywhere unaccompanied by thee? Now go instantly and search for them, and if thou find them not, be assured that on thy head shall fall the penalty."

At these words the Prince was filled with sudden foreboding, for he knew that the brothers had no love for him, and well could he see now the danger into which he had fallen. All he could do, however, was to obey; so furnishing himself with arms and a horse good for travelling, he set out in search of his brethren.

After some days employed in a fruitless quest he came to a desolate tract in the midst of which stood a castle of black marble. As he approached he

beheld at an upper window a damsel of marvellous beauty, with torn garments, dishevelled hair, and a countenance expressive of the most lively affliction, who immediately when she set eyes on him wrung her hands and waived him away crying, "Oh, fly, fly from this place of death and the monster which inhabits it! For here lives a terrible giant which feeds on human flesh, seizing all he can find. Even now in his dungeons you may hear the cries of those whom for his next meal he will devour."

"Madam," replied the Prince, "for my safety you need have no care. Only be good enough to inform me who you are and how you came to be in your present plight." "I come from Cairo," she replied, "where my birth gives me rank. And as I was travelling from thence on my road to Bagdad this monstrous brute suddenly fell upon us, and having slain my escort brought me hither a captive, to endure, if Heaven refuses me succour, things far worse than death. But though I know my own peril I will not see others perish in a vain attempt to rescue me, therefore once more I entreat you to fly before it is too late."

But even as she spoke, the giant, a horrible and gigantic monster of loathsome appearance, came in sight moving rapidly toward the palace. No sooner had he caught sight of the Prince than he rushed upon him with growls of fury, and drawing his scimitar aimed at him a blow which, had it found him, must there and then have ended the fight. The Prince, however, swerved nimbly under the stroke, and reaching his farthest, wounded the giant in the knee; then wheeling his charger about before the monster could turn on his maimed limb he attacked him from the rear, and with one fortunate blow brought him to earth. Instantly, before the giant could gather up his huge length and regain his vantage, Codadad spurred forward and with a single sweep of his sword smote off his head.

Meanwhile, all breathless above, the lady had leaned watching the contest. Now, seeing that victory was secured, she gave free vent to her joy and gratitude. "O prince of men!" she cried, "now is revealed to me the high rank

The lady advanced to meet him

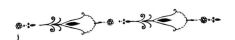 
to which thou wast born. Finish, then, thy work; take from the girdle of yonder wretch the keys of the castle and come quickly to the release of me and my fellow prisoners."

The Prince did according to her directions; as he opened the gates and entered the forecourt the lady advanced to meet him, ready, had he permitted it, to throw herself in gratitude at his feet. And now, as he beheld near at hand the beauty which had charmed him from a distance, Codadad realized how great had been his fortune, and with his whole heart rejoiced at the deliverance of one in whose nature so much virtue and grace seemed blended.

But while he was thus lost in the contemplation of her loveliness there arose from the basement of the castle a dreadful sound of crying and lamentation. "What is that?" inquired the Prince. "It is the cry of the prisoners," replied the lady, "to whom, I doubt not, the opening of the gates has betokened the monster's return. Come, therefore, quickly and relieve them of their misery." And so saying she pointed to the door which led to the place of confinement.

Thither, accompanied by the lady, went Codadad with all speed. Descending by a dark stair he came upon a vast cavern dimly lighted, around the walls of which a hundred prisoners lay chained. Instantly he set to work to loose their bonds, informing them at the same time of the death of their captor and of their freedom from all further danger. At these unexpected tidings the captives raised a cry of joy and thanksgiving; but great as was their surprise at such unexpected deliverance, greater still was that of the Prince when, on bringing them to the light, he discovered that forty-nine of the hundred whom he had released were his own brethren.

The Princes received the cordial embraces of their deliverer with little embarrassment, for the disaster into which they had fallen had caused them almost entirely to forget their original intent. Satisfied with expressing in proper terms their obligation and gratitude toward Codadad, they now joined eagerly in his survey of the castle; there upon examination they found

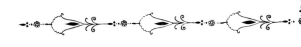

an extraordinary variety and wealth of booty, consisting for the most part of merchandise which the giant had pillaged from passing caravans, some of it actually belonging to those whom Codadad had so recently rescued.

The Prince accordingly ordered the merchants each to take what he recognized as his own; and this being done he divided the rest equally between them. The question then arose how they should remove their plunder from a place so desolately situated, where it would seem impossible to procure means of conveyance; but on a further search they found not only the camels of the merchants, but also the horses on which the Princes of Harran had ridden; and as, at their approach, the slaves who were in charge of the stables fell into headlong flight, Codadad and his companions found themselves left in undisputed possession. The merchants therefore loaded their camels, and with renewed protestations of gratitude departed on the several roads by which their avocations called them.

When they had gone Codadad's next care was to inquire of the lady in what direction she wished to travel, promising that he and the Princes would conduct her in safety to any place she might name. The lady replied, thanking him for his generous offer. "But wherever I go," said she, "it cannot be to my own country, for not only is it too far distant, but cruel misfortune has separated me from it forever. And since you have put me under so great an obligation, let me now confess the truth which before I thought prudent to conceal. My dignity of rank is far higher than that to which I recently laid claim; in me you behold a King's daughter, and if it will interest you to hear the story of my misfortunes, I shall be happy to recount it." Assured of the lively sympathy of her auditors she began as follows:

THE PRINCESS
OF
DERYABAR

MY father was the King of a city among the isles named Deryabar, and I was his only child; for, in spite of his many prayers directed to that end, Heaven had not granted him a son. And for this cause, though he bestowed upon my education all imaginable care, the sight of me remained displeasing to him. In order the better to forget his sorrow he spent his days in hunting, and so he chanced on the event which led to all our misfortunes. For one day, as he was riding unattended in the forest, night overtook him and he knew not which way to turn. Presently in the distance he perceived a light, and advancing towards it he came upon a hut within which a monstrous giant stood basting an ox that roasted before the fire. In the farther corner of the hut lay a beautiful woman with hands bound, and a face betokening the deepest affliction, while at her feet a young child, between two and three years of age, stretched up its arms and wailed without ceasing.

At this sight my father was filled with compassion, but his desire to effect her rescue was restrained for a while by fear that a failure might only make matters worse. In the meantime the giant, having drained a pitcher of wine, sat down to eat. Presently he turned himself about and addressed the lady. "Charming Princess," said he, "why will you not accept the good things which are within your reach? Only yield to me the love that I demand and you will find in me the gentlest and most considerate of lords." To these advances, however, the lady replied with resolution and courage. "Vile monster," she cried, "every time I look at you does but increase my hatred and loathing toward you. Unchangeable as the foulness of your appearance is the disgust with which you inspire me!"

These words of violent provocation were no sooner uttered than the giant, beside himself with rage, drew his sword, and seizing the lady by the hair, lifted her from the ground in preparation for the blow that would have ended all. Whereupon, seeing that not a moment was to be lost, my father drew his

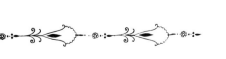

bow and let fly an arrow with so good an aim that, pierced to the heart, the giant fell dead. Immediately entering the hut my father raised the lady from the swoon into which she had fallen, and severing her bonds gave her the needed reassurance that all danger was now over. Before long he learned in answer to his inquiries that she had been wife to a chief of the Saracens, in whose service the slain giant had, on account of his great strength, occupied a position of trust. This, however, he had shamelessly betrayed; for having conceived a violent passion for his master's wife, he first persuaded the chief into an expedition which terminated in his death, and then returning in haste carried away by force not only the lady but her child also. From this degrading bondage my father's act had now saved her; but though thus relieved of immediate danger, the wife of the Saracen chief was both solitary and friendless, for not only was she too far removed from her own land to return to it unaided, but she had small hope, should she ever arrive there, of securing for her son his rightful inheritance. This being the case my father, moved with compassion, determined to adopt the child as his own; and as the lady gratefully accepted his proposal, the next day, as soon as it was light, he returned to Deryabar bringing with him mother and son.

Thus it came about that the son of a Saracen chief was brought up in my father's palace like a Prince of the blood royal; and so, on attaining to manhood, having both grace and good looks to recommend him, he came to forget the comparative lowliness of his origin, and aspiring to become my father's heir, had the presumption to demand my hand in marriage.

A claim so audacious merited the severest punishment, yet my father merely remarked that he had other views concerning me, and with so lenient a rebuke would have passed the matter by. His refusal, however, excited in the proud youth the liveliest resentment; seeing that he could not obtain his ambition by fair means he immediately entered into conspiracy, and having treacherously slain my father, caused himself to be made King in his place. Fresh from this monstrous crime he renewed his suit for my hand, and was

preparing to enforce it by violence, when the vizier, who alone of all my father's court had remained faithful to his memory, found means to convey me from the palace to a sailing vessel which was leaving harbor the same night.

Here for a time I seemed to have reached safety, but when we had been only three days at sea a violent storm arose, and the ship, driving helplessly before it, struck upon a rock and went down leaving as sole survivor the one who least wished to be spared. How I was saved I know not, nor how long I lay unfriended by the desolate shore upon which I had been cast; but scarcely had the consciousness of life returned to me when I heard a multitudinous sound of swift galloping; and presently, feeling myself lifted by men's hands, I turned and saw halting near me a troop of Arab horsemen, and at their head a youth royally arrayed and beautiful as the morning. Thus when my fortunes were at their lowest I beheld him whom Heaven had sent not only to afford me that deliverance of which I stood so much in need, but also to restore me to the rank due to my birth. For let me confess that after this young Prince had helped me with the most tender solicitude, conducting me in all honor to his own palace and there lodging me under his mother's protection, I experienced towards him a feeling of duty and gratitude such as would have made his lightest wish my law. When therefore with an ardent and ever-increasing devotion he desired me to become his bride, I could not, upon the completion of my recovery, refuse him the happiness he sought.

But the festivities of our marriage were scarcely ended, when suddenly by night the city in which we dwelt was attacked by a band of travelling marauders. The attack was so unexpected and so well planned that the town was stormed and the garrison cut to pieces before any news of the event had reached the palace. Under cover of darkness we managed to escape, and fleeing to the seashore took refuge on a small fishing boat, in which we immediately put out to sea, hoping to find in the rude winds and waves a safer shelter than our own walls had afforded us.

For two days we drifted with wind and tide, not knowing any better direction in which to turn; upon the third we perceived with relief a ship bearing down upon us, but as we watched it approach our satisfaction was soon changed to apprehension and dread, for we saw clearly that those on board were neither fishermen nor traders, but pirates. With rude shouts they boarded our small barque, and seizing my husband and myself carried us captive to their own vessel. Here the one who was their leader advanced towards me and pulled aside my veil; whereupon a great clamor instantly arose among the crew, each contending for the possession of me. The dispute upon this point grew so warm that presently they fell to fighting; and a bitter and deadly conflict was maintained till at last only a single pirate was left. This one, who now regarded himself as my owner, proceeded to inform me of what was to be my fate. "I have," he said, "a friend in Cairo who has promised me a rich reward if I can supply him with a slave, more beautiful than any of those that his harem now contains. The distinction of earning me this reward shall be yours. But tell me," he went on, turning towards the place where my husband stood bound, "who is this youth that accompanies you? Is he a lover or a brother, or only a servant?" "Sir," said I, "he is my husband." "In that case,"he replied, "out of pity we must get rid of him, for I would not afflict him needlessly with the sight of another's happiness." And so saying, he took my husband, all bound as he was, and threw him into the sea.

So great was my grief at the sight of this cruel deed, that had I not been bound myself I should undoubtedly have sought the same end to my sufferings. But for the sake of future profit the pirate took the most watchful care of me, not only so long as we were on board the ship but also when, a few days later, we came to port and there joined ourselves to a large caravan which was about to start on the road to Cairo. While thus travelling in apparent safety, we were suddenly attacked by the terrible giant who lately owned this castle. After a long and dubious conflict the pirate, and all who stood by him were slain, while I and those of the merchants who had

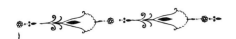

remained timorously looking on were seized, and brought hither as prisoners destined as it seemed for a fate far more lingering and terrible. The rest of my story, brave Prince, I need not here recount, since the shaping of it was so largely in your own hands, and since to you alone is owed the happiness of its conclusion.

When the Princess of Deryabar had thus finished the tale of her wanderings, Codadad hastened to assure her how deep was his sympathy in all her misfortunes. "But if you will allow yourself," he continued, "to be guided by me, your future life shall be one of safety and tranquility. You have but to come as my bride, and the King of Harran will offer you an honorable welcome to his court; while, as regards myself, my whole life shall be devoted to securing for you that happiness which your grace and noble qualities prove that you deserve. And that you may not regard this proposal as too presumptuous, I have now to inform you, and also these Princes, concerning my birth and rank. For I, too, am a son of the King of Harran, born to him at the court of Samaria by his wife the Princess Pirouzè, whom he had sent unjustly into banishment."

This declaration on the part of Codadad so accorded with the inclinations of the Princess that she at once yielded her consent, and as the castle was full of provisions suitable for the occasion, preparations were made first to solemnize the marriage, and then for all together to set forth on the return journey to Harran. As for the Princes, though they received Codadad's news with every outward protestation of joy, they were in fact more filled with apprehension and jealousy than before, for they could not but fear that his favor with the King would be greatly increased and become far more dangerous to their interests when the true facts of his birth were revealed. No sooner, therefore, had Codadad and the Princess passed to their wedding, than his brethren entered into a conspiracy to slay him; and at the first halt upon the homeward journey, taking advantage of the lack of protection

which a tent affords, they came upon their brother by night, and stabbing him in a hundred places as he lay asleep, left him for dead in the arms of his bride. They then broke up the camp and returned with all haste to the city of Harran, where, with a falsely invented tale, they excused themselves to the King for their long absence.

In the meantime Codadad lay so spent by loss of blood that there remained in him no sign of life. The Princess his wife, distraught with grief, had already given him up for dead. "O Heaven," she cried, bathing his body with her tears, "why am I thus ever condemned to bring on others disaster and death, and why for a second time have I been deprived of the one I was about to love?"

As thus she continued to cry in piteous lamentation, and to gaze on the senseless form lying before her, she thought that she perceived on the lips a faint motion of breath. At once her hope revived, and springing to her feet she ran instantly in the direction of the nearest village, hoping to find there a surgeon or one that had skill in the binding of wounds. Returning after a time with the aid that she had summoned she found to her grief the place where Codadad had lain left vacant, nor was there any trace or indication of the fate which had overtaken him.

Overwhelmed by this final catastrophe, and believing that some wild beast must have devoured him, she suffered herself to be led away by the surgeon, who, in pity for one so greatly afflicted, placed her under the shelter of his own roof, and lavished upon her every mark of consideration and respect. So, when she had sufficiently recovered from her grief to find utterance, he gathered from her own lips all the circumstances of her story, her name and rank, the high and valiant deeds of the Prince her husband, and the base ingratitude of his brethren. And perceiving that her grief and sufferings had so robbed her of the desire of life that without some end on which to direct her will she would presently pass into a decline, the surgeon endeavored to arouse her to the pursuit of that just vengeance which the

A city among the Isles named Deryabar

murder of her husband had earned. "Do not," he said, "let the death of so noble a Prince become a benefit to his enemies. Let us go together to the King of Harran, and make known to him the guilt of these wicked brethren. For surely the name of Codadad should live in story; but if you, whose honor he saved, now sink under your affliction his name perishes with you, and you have not retrieved your debt."

These words roused the Princess from her deep despondency; forming her resolution on the surgeon's advice, she arose instantly and prepared herself for the journey, and with such haste and diligence did she pursue her project that within two days she and her companion arrived at the city of Harran.

Here strange news awaited them; for at all the caravanseries it was told how lately there had come to the city an exiled wife of the King, Princess Pirouzè by name, inquiring for news of her lost son; and how, as now appeared, this son had already been under a feigned designation at his father's court, and after performing many exploits and deeds of heroism had disappeared none knew where. Forty-nine sons had the King by different wives, but all these, it was declared, he would willingly put to death so that Codadad might be restored to him.

Now when the Princess of Deryabar heard this, she said, "I will go to the Queen Pirouzè and make known to her the fate of her son, and when we have wept together and drawn comfort from each other in our grief then we will go before the King, and demand vengeance on the murderers." But the surgeon said, "Have a care what you do; for if the Princes of Harran learn of your arrival, they will not rest till they have done to you as they did to your husband. Let us therefore proceed with secrecy, so as to ensure safety, and do not on any account let your presence here be known till the King has been thoroughly informed of the whole matter." Then leaving the Princess in a place discreetly chosen, he went forth into the streets and began to direct his steps towards the palace. Presently he was met by a lady mounted upon a mule richly caparisoned, and behind her followed a great troop of guards and

attendants. As she approached the populace ran out of their houses and stood in rows to see her go by, and when she passed all bowed down with their faces to the earth. The surgeon inquired of a beggar standing near whether this was one of the King's wives. "Yes, brother," replied the beggar, "and the best of them all; for she is the mother of Prince Codadad, whom, now that he is lost, all hold in love and reverence. And thus each day she goes to the mosque to hear the prayers which the King has ordered for her son's safe return."

Seeing his course now clear the surgeon went and stood at the door of the mosque, waiting for the Queen's departure, and when she came forth with all her attendants he plucked one of them by the sleeve and said to him, "If the Queen would have news of her son, Prince Codadad, let her send for the stranger who will be found waiting at the door of her palace." So, as soon as Pirouzè had returned to her apartments, the slave went in and gave his mistress the message. Then she sent in all haste for the surgeon to be brought before her. And the surgeon prostrated himself and said, "O Queen, let not the grief of the tidings which I bear be visited upon me but on them that were the cause of it." And she answered him, "Have peace, and say on!" So he told her, as has been here set forth, the full story of all the courage and prowess of Codadad, and of his generosity towards his brethren, also of his marriage to the Princess of Deryabar and of what followed after. But when he came to speak of the slaying of her son, the tender mother, as though receiving in her own body the strokes of the murderers, fell forward upon the ground, and there for a while lay motionless without sign of life. When however the surgeon, aided by her women, had restored her to consciousness, then Pirouzè, putting aside all personal grief, set her mind upon the accomplishment of the duty which now lay before her. "Go instantly," she said, "and tell the Princess of Deryabar that the King will shortly receive her with all the honor due to her rank. As for yourself, be assured that your services will be remembered."

The ship struck upon a rock

Hardly had the surgeon departed, when the King himself entered, and the sight of his Queen's deep affliction at once informed him that something dreadful must have occurred. "Alas," she cried, "our son no longer exists, nor is it even possible to pay to his body those last rites which were due to his rank and virtue, for stricken by treacherous hands and left to perish unprotected he has fallen a prey to wild beasts so that not a trace of him remains." She then proceeded to inform her husband of all the horrible circumstances which the surgeon had narrated.

But before she had ended the King became so transported with rage and grief that he could no longer delay his just vengeance. Repairing in haste to the hall of audience, where courtiers and suitors stood waiting, he summoned to him his grand vizier with so much fury of countenance that all trembled for their lives. "Go instantly," he cried, "arrest all the Princes, and convey them under a strong guard to the prison assigned for murderers!" The vizier, not daring to question an order so terribly uttered, went forth and fulfilled the King's command with all speed. On his return to the palace for the presentation of his report, a further order almost equally surprising awaited him. The King described to him a certain inn lying in a poor quarter of the city. "Go there," said he, "take with you slaves and high attendants, a white mule from the royal stables, and a guard of honor, and bring here with all the respect due to her rank the young Princess whom you shall find there."

The vizier, with revived spirits, went forth to fulfill this second mission, so much more agreeable to him than the first; and presently there arose from the streets leading to the palace the acclamations of the populace because of the magnificence and splendor which announced the arrival of the unknown Princess. The King, as a token of respect, stood waiting at the palace gates to receive her, and taking her hand he led her to the apartments of the Queen Pirouzè. Here at the meeting of mother and wife a scene of the most tender and heartrending affliction took place. The King himself was so moved by it that he had not the heart to refuse to them any request. So when they came

and besought for the absent those funeral honors which under other circumstances would have been his due, he gave orders for a dome of marble to be erected on the plain by which the city of Harran lies surrounded. And with such speed was the work put in hand, and so large was the number of men employed upon it, that within three days the entire building was completed.

On the following day the obsequies began. All was done with the greatest solemnity and splendor. First came the King attended by his vizier and all the officers and lords of his palace; and entering the tomb, in which lay an effigy of Codadad, they seated themselves on carpets of mourning bordered with gold. Then followed the chiefs of the army mounted upon horses and bewailing the loss of him who had led them to victory; behind these came old men upon black mules, with long robes and flowing beards; and after these maidens on white horses, with heads unveiled, bearing in their hands baskets of precious stones. Now when these had approached and encircled the dome three times, then the King rose up to speak the dismissal of the dead. Touching with his brow the tomb whereon the effigy lay, he cried in a loud voice, "O my dear son, O light of mine eyes, O joy that is lost to me forever." After him all the lords and the chiefs and the elders came and prostrated themselves in like manner; and when the ceremony was ended the doors of the tomb were shut and all the people returned to the city.

Now after this there was prayer and fasting in the mosque for eight days, and on the ninth the King gave orders that the Princes were to be beheaded. But meanwhile the neighboring powers, whose arms the King of Harran had defeated, as soon as they heard that Codadad was dead, banded themselves together in strong alliance, and with a great army began to advance upon the city. Then the King caused the execution to be postponed, and making a hasty levy of his forces went forth to meet the enemy in the open plain. And there battle was joined with such valor and determination on both sides that for a time the issue remained doubtful. Nevertheless, because the men of

Harran were fewer in number, they began to be surrounded by their enemies; but at the very moment when all seemed lost they saw in the distance a large body of horsemen advancing at the charge; and while both combatants were yet uncertain of their purpose, these fell furiously and without warning upon the ranks of the allies, and throwing them into sudden disorder, drove them in rout from the field.

With the success of their arms thus established the two leaders of the victorious forces advanced to meet each other in the presence of the whole army, and great was the joy and astonishment of the King when he discovered in the leader of the lately arrived troop his lost son Codadad. The Prince, for his part, was equally delighted to find in his father's welcome the recognition for which he had yearned.

When the long transport of their meeting embrace was over, the Prince, as they began to converse, saw with surprise how much was already known to the King of past events. "What?" he inquired, "has one of my brothers awakened to his guilt, and confessed that which I had meant should remain a secret?" "Not so," replied the King, "from the Princess of Deryabar alone have I learned the truth. For it was she who came to demand vengeance for the crime which your brothers would still have concealed."

At this unexpected news of the safety of the Princess and of her arrival at his father's court, Codadad's joy was beyond words, and was greatly increased when he heard of his mother's reinstatement in the King's favor with the honor and dignity due to her rank. He now began to perceive how events had shaped themselves in his absence, and how the King had already become informed of the bond that existed between them. As for the rest of his adventures, together with the circumstance which had led to his disappearance and supposed death, they were soon explained. For when the Princess had left Codadad in her desperate search for aid, there chanced that way a travelling pedlar; and he, finding the youth apparently deserted and dying of his wounds, took pity on him, and placing him upon his mule bore

him to his own house. There with medicinal herbs and simple arts unknown in the palaces of kings he had accomplished a cure which others would have thought impossible, so that in a short time Codadad's strength was completely restored. Thereupon the Prince, impatient for reunion with those whom he loved, bestowed on the pedlar all the wealth that he possessed, and immediately set forth toward the city of Harran.

On the road news reached him of the fresh outbreak of hostilities, followed by the invasion of his father's territory. Passing from village to village he roused and armed the inhabitants, and by the excellence of his example made such soldiers of them that they were able in the fortunate moment of their arrival to decide the issue of the conflict and give victory to the King's arms.

"And now, sire," said the Prince in conclusion, "I have only one request to make: since in the event all things have turned out so happily, I beg you to pardon my brothers in order that I may prove to them in the future how groundless were the resentment and jealousy that they felt toward me."

These generous sentiments drew tears from the King's eyes and removed from his mind all doubt as to the wisdom of the resolution he had been forming. Immediately before the assembled army he declared Codadad his heir, and, as an act of grace to celebrate his son's return, gave orders for the Princes to be released. He then led Codadad with all speed to the palace, where Pirouzè and her daughter-in-law were anxiously awaiting them.

In the joy of that meeting the Prince and his wife were repaid a thousand-fold for all the griefs and hardships they had undergone: and their delight in each other's society remained so great that in all the world no happiness has been known to equal it. The Princes half died of shame when the means by which their pardon had been procured was revealed to them; but before long the natural insensibility of their characters reasserted itself and they recovered.

ALADDIN AND THE
MAGIC LAMP

ONCE upon a time, in a far city of Cathay, there dwelt a poor tailor who had an only son named Aladdin. This boy was a born ne'er-do-well, and persistently resisted all his father's efforts to teach him a trade by means of which he would be able in future to earn a livelihood. Aladdin would sooner play at knuckle-bones in the gutter with others as careless as himself than he would set his mind to honest business; and, as to obeying his parents in the smallest matter, it was not in his nature. Such was this boy Aladdin, and yet—so remarkable is the favor of fate—he was strangely predestined for great things.

Stricken with grief because of the waywardness and idle conduct of his son the father fell ill and died, and the mother found great difficulty in supporting herself, to say nothing of the worthless Aladdin as well. While she wore the flesh off her bones in the endeavor to obtain a meager subsistence Aladdin would amuse himself with his fellow urchins of the street, only returning home to his meals. In this way he continued until he was fourteen years of age, when his extraordinary destiny took him by the hand, and led him, step by step, through adventures so wonderful that words can scarce describe them.

One day he was playing in the gutter with his ragged companions, as was his wont, when a Moorish Dervish came by, and, catching sight of Aladdin's face, suddenly stopped and approached him. This Dervish was a sorcerer who had discovered many hidden secrets by his black art; in fact, he was on the track of one now; and, by the look on his face as he scrutinized Aladdin's features, it seemed that the boy was closely connected with his quest.

The Dervish beckoned to one of the urchins and asked him who Aladdin was, who his father was, and indeed all about him. Having thus learned the whole history of the boy and his family the Dervish gave his informer some coins and sent him away to spend them. Then he approached Aladdin and

said to him, "Boy, I seem to recognize in thee a family likeness. Art thou not the tailor's son?" Aladdin answered him that he was, and added that his father was dead.

On hearing this the Dervish cried out with grief and embraced Aladdin, weeping bitterly. The boy was surprised at this and inquired the cause of such sorrow. "Alas!" replied the Dervish with tears running down his cheeks, "my fate is an unhappy one. Boy, I have come from a distant country to find my brother, to look upon his face again, and to cheer and comfort him; and now thou tellest me he is dead." He took Aladdin's face in his hands and gazed searchingly upon it as he continued: "Boy, I recognize my brother's features in thine; and, now that he is dead, I will find comfort in thee."

Aladdin looked up at him in wonder, for he had never been told that he had an uncle; indeed, he was inclined to doubt the truth of the matter; but, when the Dervish took ten pieces of gold from his purse and placed them in his hand, all doubt was out of the question, and he rejoiced at having found so rich an uncle. The Dervish then asked him concerning his mother and begged him to show him the way to her house. And, when Aladdin had showed him, he gave the boy more gold and said, "Give this to thy mother with my blessing, and say that her brother-in-law, who has been absent forty years, has returned and will visit her tomorrow to weep with her over the place where his brother is buried." With this he departed, and Aladdin ran to his mother to tell her the news.

The next day the Dervish sought Aladdin in the street where he had seen him the day before, and found him there among his disreputable friends. Taking him aside he kissed him and embraced him; then, placing ten gold pieces in his hand, he said, "Hasten now to thy mother and give her these gold pieces and say that her brother-in-law would come to dine at her house this night."

So Aladdin left him and ran home to his mother with the gold pieces and the message. Then the widow busied herself and prepared for the coming of

this new-found relative. She bought rich food, and borrowed from the neighbors such dishes, utensils and table linen as she required. When the supper was ready, and the widow was about to send Aladdin to hasten the guest, the Dervish entered, followed by a slave bearing fruit and wine, which he set down, and then went his way. The Dervish, weeping bitterly, saluted the widow and immediately fell to asking questions about the departed.

Then, when he was comforted and they all sat at supper together, the Dervish turned to Aladdin and asked him if he knew any art or trade. At this Aladdin hung his head, and, as he was too ashamed to answer, his mother dried her tears and answered for him. "Alack!" she said, "he is nothing but an idler. He spends his time as thou didst find him, playing with ragamuffins in the street, and is never at home except at meal times. And I—I am an old woman and ugly through toil and hardship, and grief at his behavior. O my brother-in-law! It is he who should provide for me, not I for him."

"I am grieved to hear this of thee," said the Dervish, turning to Aladdin; "for thou art no longer a child. Wouldst thou like to be a merchant?" he asked. "If so I will give thee a shop with all kinds of merchandise, and thou shalt buy and sell and get gain, and rise to a position of importance."

At this Aladdin clapped his hands with glee, and his mother was rejoiced. And she chid her boy for his own good, and counselled him straitly to obey his uncle in all things. The Dervish also gave Aladdin much sound advice on the conduct of trade, so that the boy's head was bursting with buying and selling, and he could not sleep that night for dreams of rich stuffs, and bales of merchandise. At last, when the Dervish arose and took his departure, promising to return for Aladdin on the morrow and take him to buy his merchant's dress, the wizard felt that he had proved himself undoubtedly the best of brothers-in-law, and the best of uncles.

True to his word the Dervish came on the morrow, and Aladdin, holding him affectionately by the hand, went with him forth to the market. There they entered a shop full of the finest materials, and the Dervish asked to be

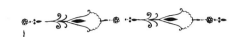

shown some dresses such as a wealthy merchant might wear. The owner of the shop laid a great variety before him and the Dervish said, "Now, my son, choose what dress you like." This delicate favor of choice pleased Aladdin greatly, for it seemed that he had now at last reached the age of discretion. He picked out one that he liked, and the Dervish paid the price without any attempt at bargaining. Then they went together to the Hammam, and, when they had bathed and rested, Aladdin clothed himself in his new dress and came forth in great delight, kissing his uncle's hand and thanking him again and again.

After they had rested the Dervish suggested a walk, and he led Aladdin through garden after garden until they came to the confines of the city, beyond which stood a high hill. "Shall we return, O my uncle?" said Aladdin, who was in no mood for climbing the hill. "There are no more gardens outside the city." "Nay," replied the Dervish, "on the hillside is the loveliest garden of all. Bear up, my son, and be a man; we shall soon be there." And, as they went, he beguiled the boy with anecdotes, so that Aladdin forgot both the length of the way and his weariness.

At last they came to a place on the hillside where the Dervish paused and looked about him, saying to himself, "This is the spot I have journeyed so far to find." But to Aladdin he said, "Rest here awhile, O my son, and, when thou art refreshed, gather some wood and we will make a fire; then, if thou wish to see a most wonderful thing, I will show thee that which will take thy breath away."

At this Aladdin's curiosity was excited, and, with no thought of resting, he began at once to gather wood. When he had collected a sufficient quantity the Dervish lighted the fire, and, taking from his wallet a little box, drew some fine powder from it and scattered it over the fire, uttering an incantation. Immediately, amid rumblings of thunder, the earth reeled and opened. At this Aladdin fled in terror, but the Dervish, powerless to effect his

purpose without the boy's aid, flew after him in a rage, and smote him over the head, so that he fell to the ground stunned.

When, presently, he regained his senses, he sat up and cried out, "What have I done, O my uncle, that thou shouldst strike me?" "Nay, my son," replied the Dervish, "I intended not to hurt thee. Come, now, be a man, and obey my wishes if thou wouldst see the wonderful things that I will show thee." With such words as these he banished Aladdin's fears and smoothed him over. Then he directed him to the opening in the earth, where there was revealed a slab of marble with a brass ring let into it. The Dervish stooped and began to draw figures upon the ground, saying as he did so, "Obey me, Aladdin, in all that I say, for so thou shalt become richer than all the kings of the earth. Know, O my son, that beyond that slab of stone lies vast treasure which none but thee can acquire and use. Therefore, advance, my son, and take the brass ring in thy hand and lift the slab from its place; for it is predestined that thou art the only one on this earth that hath the power to do this thing." And Aladdin, stirred to great wonder by the words of the Dervish, would have done his bidding with alacrity, but, on looking at the marble slab, he saw that it was far too heavy for him.

"Never can I raise that alone, O my uncle," he said. "Wilt thou not help me?" "Nay," answered the Dervish, "it will yield to no hand but thine. Grasp the ring and repeat the names of as many of thine ancestors as thou canst remember, beginning with thy father and mother; for thine ancestors are my ancestors, O my son! By this the stone will come away quite easily in thy hand as if it were a feather. Am I not thine uncle, and have I not said it? And did I not cleave the hillside with my incantations? Wherefore, pluck up courage, and forget not that all the riches beyond that stone are for thee."

Thus encouraged Aladdin advanced to the stone, repeating the names of all the ancestors he could remember; and, taking hold of the ring, lifted the heavy slab from its place with perfect ease, and threw it aside. Then within the aperture lay revealed a stairway of twelve steps leading into a passage.

While Aladdin was gazing at this wonder the Dervish took a ring from his finger and placed it upon the middle finger of the boy's right hand, saying impressively as he did so, "Listen to me, O my son! Fear nothing in what I am about to bid thee do, for this ring will be thy protection in all dangers and against all evils. If thou shouldst find thyself in evil case thou hast only to—but of that I will tell thee presently. What is more important now is this. In order to come at the treasure, O my son, steady thyself and listen attentively, and see to it that thou fail not a word of these my instructions. Go down the steps and traverse the passage to the end, where thou wilt find a chamber divided into four parts, each containing four vessels of gold. Touch not these on thy life, for if so much as the fringe of thy robe cometh in contact with any of them, thou wilt immediately be turned into stone. Linger not to gaze upon them, but pass right through to the end, where thou wilt find a door. Open this, repeating again the names of thine ancestors, when lo, thou wilt behold a beautiful garden before thee. Take the pathway that is ready for thy feet and proceed forty-nine cubits until thou comest to an alcove, where is set a stairway of forty-nine steps. Look not to ascend that stairway: it is not for thee nor me; but direct thine attention to a lamp hanging above the alcove. Take it from its fastening, and pour out the oil therein; then put it in thy breast securely, and retrace thy steps to me. Is it clear to thee, my son?"

"O my uncle, it is quite clear," replied Aladdin, and he repeated the instructions he had received. "Pull thy wits together then, my son," said the Dervish, well pleased; "and descend, for verily thou art a man of mettle, and not a child. Yea, thou, and thou only, art the rightful owner of all this great treasure. Come now!"

Filled with courage from the wizard's words, and enticed by the dazzle of untold riches, Aladdin descended the twelve steps and passed through the fourfold chamber with the utmost care lest he should touch any of the golden jars therein with so much as the fringe of his garment. When he came to the door at the far end he paused to repeat the names of his ancestors, and

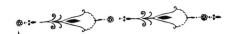

opened it; then, lo, before him lay a beautiful garden where the trees were laden with many colored fruit, while sweet-voiced birds sang in the branches. He took the pathway that lay before his feet, and, as he followed it, he looked up and noticed that the trees bore, not fruit as he had supposed, but sparkling jewels flashing with many colors.

But Aladdin, though dazzled by the glitter, thought these sparkling things were but colored glass; and it was for such that he plucked them with boyish delight until his pockets were full. "These are lovely things to play with," he said, and proceeded to fill his girdle also.

As he made his way along the garden path, plucking the bright jewels as he went, he caught sight of the alcove at the far end, and, remembering his uncle's instructions, hastened towards it. There was the stairway of forty-nine steps, and there, hanging from a crystal beam, was the Lamp. He paused, looking up at it. How should he reach it? His uncle had said that the stairway was neither for Aladdin nor for himself, and yet he saw at a glance that the only way of reaching the Lamp was by mounting seven steps of the stairway. He hesitated, then, concluding that the Lamp was the whole object of his quest, and that he must reach it at all costs, he ventured. With some misgivings he mounted the seven steps and, reaching out, took the Lamp from its fastening and descended with it. Then, emptying out the oil, he placed it securely in his bosom, saying, "Now, as my uncle said to me, with this Lamp in my bosom all is mine!"

As Aladdin was returning along the pathway among the trees, laden with the precious jewels, fear assailed him lest his uncle would be angry at his delay, for it was borne in upon him that no great delight can come to a mortal without his having to suffer for it. Whereupon he hastened his footsteps, and, passing through the fourfold chamber without touching the golden jars—for the fear of that was still upon him—he arrived quickly at the foot of the stairway of twelve steps. Heavily weighted as he was with the jewels and the Lamp he proceeded to mount the stairs at a run. But the jewels grew heavier,

and the Lamp weighed upon his bosom, so that he was exhausted by the time he was halfway up. Kneeling on the seventh step he looked up and saw the Dervish urging him on with the greatest impatience.

"Bear with me, O my uncle," he said. "I am heavily weighted and am out of breath. I will soon come to thee." Then he climbed three steps and one step more, and sank exhausted before the last, which was far higher than the others. The jewels and the Lamp oppressed him with heaviness and he could not mount that last step. "O my uncle, give me thy hand and help me up," he cried. But the wizard dare not touch him, for so the spell of fate was worded and he must abide by it. "Nay," he called down, "thou art man enough! It is the Lamp that hampers thee. Reach up and place it on the ledge here; then thou canst mount easily thyself."

The Dervish held out his hand expectantly for the Lamp and his eyes glittered. Aladdin saw the evil light in them, and, having some mother wit, replied, "O my uncle, the Lamp is no weight at all; it is simply that I am exhausted and this step is too high for me. Give me thy hand and help me up." "Give me the Lamp!" cried the Dervish, holding his hand out for it, and beginning to rage. "Place it on the ledge before thee, and then I will help thee up." "Nay," returned Aladdin, growing obstinate, "if thou wilt not give me thy hand I will not give thee the Lamp, for it is in my thoughts that thou wantest the Lamp more than thou wantest me."

This enraged the Dervish to a point beyond control, and he said within himself, "If I get not the Lamp then may it perish with him!" And, taking a box from his wallet, he threw some powder on the embers of the fire, muttering curses and incantations as he did so. Immediately a flame shot up, and its many tongues went hither and thither, licking the air. The earth shuddered and groaned with a hollow thunder; then the marble slab closed of itself over the aperture, the hillside rushed together above it, and all was as before, save that Aladdin was sealed within that cavern without hope of escape.

Long and loud did Aladdin call to his supposed uncle to save him from a living death; but there was no answer to his cries, and, at last, when he was almost exhausted, he took counsel of himself and plainly saw the truth of the matter. The Dervish was no uncle of his, but a cunning wizard who had made a catspaw of him to secure treasure which, by the laws of magic and destiny, he was powerless to come at in any other way. The whole thing, from the very beginning, was a trick; and he saw it clearly now that it was too late. The way out was sealed, and the darkness pressed heavily upon him. Frantic with the desire to escape from this dungeon he thought of the garden and the stairway in the alcove; but, when he had groped his way to the end of the passage, he found the door closed, and all his efforts failed to open it. The names of his ancestors were of no avail against the magic of the Dervish. At this he wept loudly, and continued to weep throughout the night, until his rage and despair were spent. At last he sank down exhausted on the lowest step of the stairway by which he had first descended, and, feeling himself utterly abandoned by man, he raised his hands to God, praying for deliverance from his calamity.

Now, while he was holding his hands in supplication, he felt the ring upon his middle finger—the ring which the Dervish had placed there saying, "In whatever difficulty thou mayst find thyself this ring will be thy protection; thou hast only to—but of that I will tell thee later." The Dervish had perhaps given him the ring to gain his confidence, and had purposely omitted to reveal its secret. But now, in answer to Aladdin's prayer, the power of the ring was revealed as if by the merest chance; for, when he felt the ring, he looked at it; and, seeing a light from the jewel therein, he breathed upon it and rubbed it with his palm to increase its lustre. No sooner had he done this when, lo, the Slave of the Ring appeared, and gathered shape before him, first in a luminous haze, and then, gradually, in clearer and clearer contour.

"Ask what thou wilt, and it shall be done," said the apparition; "for know that I am the Slave of the Ring and the slave of him on whose finger my master placed the ring."

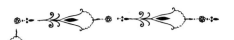

Aladdin, seeing before him an Efrite after the order of those invoked by the Lord Suleiman, was terrified, and his tongue stuck to the roof of his mouth, so that he could not speak. But the Efrite reassured him with kindly speech. "Thou hast only to ask," he said, "and thy wish will be fulfilled; for, since my master's ring is on thy hand, I am thy servant."

At this Aladdin took heart, and, having considered his wish, resolved to put the matter to test. "O Slave of the Ring!" he said, "my wish is that thou take me from this dungeon and place me in the light of day where the sun shines and the breezes blow—if indeed it *is* day, for here have I been for many, many hours."

Scarcely had he spoken the words when there was a clap of thunder. The cavern opened, and, by some mysterious power, he was conveyed through the opening. Then, when he sat up and looked around him, he was in the light of day upon the hillside, and everything was as it had been when he and the Dervish had first reached the spot.

Aladdin marvelled greatly at this, and said within himself, "I wonder if it was all a dream!" But, when he looked at the ring upon his finger and felt the Lamp and the jewel-fruit he had gathered from the trees in the garden, he knew it was not a dream. Besides, there was the spot where the fire had been; and it was now but a heap of grey ashes on the ground. Turning himself about, he saw the path by which they had ascended, and the gardens stretching below. Nothing had changed. The side of the hill which the Dervish by his magic had opened for his entrance, and the Slave of the Ring had now closed up behind him, was as it had been when he first saw it.

Seeing that he was safe and sound in the outer world, Aladdin fell on his knees and gave thanks to the most High for his deliverance from a terrible death. Then straightway he arose and took the path that led down the hillside and through the gardens of the city in the direction of his home. At length, with wearied body, but elated mind, he reached the doorway of his dwelling, and, entering, found his mother weeping.

"Where hast thou been, my son?" she cried. "All night long I lay awake, anxious for thee; and now it is again near nightfall, and thou comest like one about to die. Where hast thou been, and where is thine uncle?"

But Aladdin could not answer her. What with utter weariness, and the joy of gaining his home once more, he fell in a swoon at her feet. Quickly she dashed water on his face and restored him. Then, when she had made him eat, she inquired gently what had befallen him.

"O my mother," said Aladdin, "how much thou art to blame! Thou gavest me over to a devil of a sorcerer who tried, by his evil arts, to compass my ruin." And thus, having vented his anger at the false conduct of the Dervish, he proceeded to tell his mother, first about the lamp and the jewel-fruit, then about all that had happened on the hillside, from the opening of the earth by a magic spell, to the closing of it again, and his subsequent escape through the Slave of the Ring.

Then Aladdin took the Lamp and the precious stones from his bosom and placed them before his mother, although neither knew why the Lamp had been so coveted by the Dervish, or that the stones were more valuable than any possessed by kings.

Now, neither Aladdin nor his mother had rested for two days and two nights, so that, exhausted at length with weeping and with heaping maledictions on the Dervish, they slept; and, when they awoke, it was about noon of the following day. Aladdin's first words on pulling his wits together were to the effect that he was hungry. "Nay, O my son," replied his mother, "there is nothing to eat in the house, for thou didst eat yesterday all that there was. But stay, I have some spinning that is ready for the market. I will take and sell it and buy some food."

She was busying herself about this when Aladdin suddenly called out to her, "Mother! bring me the Lamp, and I will take and sell that; it will fetch more than the spinning." Now, although Aladdin and his mother knew that the Dervish had greatly coveted the Lamp, they both imagined that he had

some strange reason of his own for this; and, as the Lamp was an article that would command a ready sale, the mother quickly agreed to Aladdin's proposal and brought the Lamp to him in answer to his call. On regarding it closely, however, she observed that it was very dirty. Well knowing that it would fetch a better price if it were clean and bright, she set to work to polish it with some fine sand; when lo, as soon as she started to rub the Lamp, the air before her danced and quivered and a chill gasp of wind smote her in the face. Then, looking up, she saw, towering above her, a being monstrous and terrible, with a fierce face in which gleamed fiery eyes beneath frowning brows. She gazed at this apparition in fear and astonishment, for she knew it was surely a powerful Efrite such as were under the power of the Lord Suleiman. Then the being spoke: "Thou hast invoked me; what is thy wish?" But she only gazed at him, dumb with terror. Again the awful being spoke: "Thou hast summoned me, for I am the Slave of the Lamp which is in thy hand. What is thy desire?" At this the poor woman could no longer endure her fear, and, with a cry, she fell in a swoon.

Aladdin had heard the Efrite's words and had hastened to his mother's side. He had already seen the power of the Slave of the Ring, and he guessed that now the Slave of the Lamp had appeared, and was ready to do the bidding of the one who held the Lamp. So he quickly took it from his mother's hand, and, standing before the Efrite, plucked up courage and said, "I desire food, O Slave of the Lamp! the finest food that ever was set before a king."

No sooner had he spoken than the Efrite vanished, but only to reappear immediately, bearing a rich tray of solid silver, on which were twelve golden dishes with fruits and meats of various kinds. There were also flagons of wine and silver goblets. As Aladdin stared in amazement at this magnificent repast the Efrite set the tray down before him and vanished in a flash. Then Aladdin turned to his mother and dashed cold water on her face, and held perfumes to her nostrils until she regained consciousness and sat up. And when she beheld

Aladdin in the Cave

the sumptuous repast set out upon the golden dishes she was greatly astonished, and imagined that the Sultan had sent it from his palace. But Aladdin, who was very hungry, fell to eating heartily; and, while persuading his mother to eat, he would tell her nothing.

It was not until they had satisfied their hunger, and placed the remainder aside for the morrow, that Aladdin informed her what had happened. Then she questioned him, saying, "O my son, was not this the same Efrite that appeared to thee when thou wast in the cavern?" "Nay," he answered. "That was the Slave of the Ring; this was the Slave of the Lamp." "At all events," said she, "it was a terrible monster that nearly caused my death through fear. Promise me, O my son, that thou wilt have naught further to do with the Ring and the Lamp. Cast them from thee, for the Holy Prophet hath told us to have no traffic with devils."

"Nay, nay, O my mother," protested Aladdin; "it were wiser to keep them, for did not the Slave of the Ring deliver me from death? and has not the Slave of the Lamp brought us delicious food when we were hungry?" "That may be so," replied his mother, "but hear my words, my son; no good thing can come of these dealings with accursed spirits, and it were better for thee to have died in the cavern than to invoke their aid." And thus she pleaded with him to cast away the Ring and the Lamp, for she was sore afraid of the power of the Evil One. But Aladdin would not undertake to do this, although, in respect for her wishes, he agreed to conceal the objects so that she might never need to look upon them. He also agreed to invoke neither of the Efrites again, unless it were a case of dire necessity. And with this his mother had to rest content.

Mother and son continued to live on the food that remained, until, in a few days, it was all gone. Then Aladdin took up one of the dishes from the tray, and, not knowing that it was of pure gold, went out to sell it and buy food with the proceeds. In the market he came to the shop of a fair-dealing merchant. When Aladdin showed him the dish of gold he took it, and weighed it on the scales. "My son," he said, "here is the price if thou wouldst sell."

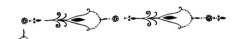 

He counted out seventy gold pieces and handed them to Aladdin, who took them and thanked the merchant heartily for his honesty. And thereafter he brought the remaining dishes, and at last the tray, to that merchant, and received from him their full value; so that Aladdin and his mother were placed above want and in a comfortable position for people of their station in life.

During this time Aladdin had changed his ways greatly. He no longer consorted with the ragamuffins of the street but selected for his friends men of standing and integrity. Often he would watch the jewellers at their work, and the goods they handled; and, through knowledge thus acquired, he began to suspect that the jewel-fruit he had gathered in the garden of the cavern was not glass, as he had imagined, but real gems. By this and that, and by comparing and asking questions, he came at length to the certainty that he actually possessed the richest jewels in all the earth. The smallest among them was bigger and more sparkling by far than the largest and finest he could see in any jeweller's shop.

One day he was in the jeweller's market, taking note of things, when a herald came by, crying to all people: "Take heed! By command of the Sultan, King of the Age and Lord of the Earth, let all doors be closed, and let none come forth from shop or dwelling on pain of instant death, for the Sultan's daughter, Bedr-el-Budur cometh to the bath! Take heed!"

Hastening to the Hammam he secreted himself behind the door so that, unobserved himself, he might see her when she came in. And presently the Sultan's daughter arrived; and, as she entered, she lifted the veil from her face, so that Aladdin saw her features clearly.

What a wondrous beauty was there! The witchery of her eyes! The ivory of her skin! The jet of her glossy tresses! These, and the swaying of her graceful body as she walked, caused Aladdin's heart to turn to water and then to spring wildly into flame.

Like one walking in a dream Aladdin went home and sat him down in dejection of spirit. For a long time he answered not his mother's questions as to what ailed him, but continued like one who had beheld a vision so lovely that it had deprived him of his senses. At last, however, he looked up, and said, "O my mother, know that until today I had believed that all women were of thy fashion of face, but now I find they are not; for today I saw the Sultan's daughter, and she is more beautiful than all others on earth." And Aladdin told her how he had hidden behind the door of the Hammam, so that, when Bedr-el-Budur had entered and lifted her veil, he had seen her clearly and how, on that, a great love had leapt up in his heart and filled him to the exclusion of all else. "And there is no rest for me," he concluded, "until I win the Lady Bedr-el-Budur, and make her my wife."

At these daring words Aladdin's mother regarded him sharply, with fear on her face. "Art thou mad, my son?" she cried. "Nay, O my mother," he answered, "I am not mad. But, as I risked my life to see her, so will I risk it again to win her; for, without her, life is of no account to me. I will go to the Sultan and ask him to give me the lovely Bedr-el-Budur for my lawful wife."

Seeing his determination his mother was sore afraid, and knew not what to do. For a long time she reasoned with him anxiously, pointing out what a scandal it would be for the son of a poor tailor to aspire to the Sultan's daughter.

These arguments, and more, his mother put before him; but Aladdin shook his head at all of them, and remained firm in his determination. "And further, O my mother," he said, "I wish now that thou go thyself to the Sultan and put my request to him, for am I not thy child? And is it not thy duty to perform this office for me?"

"O my son," she cried in despair, "wilt thou bring me into thy madness? I, a poor woman, of humble birth, to go in to the Sultan and demand the princess for my son! Besides, O my son, how shall I even gain access to the Sultan's presence for this purpose without bearing a rich gift to offer him?"

"Mother," answered Aladdin, "thy words have served me well, for they have called to my recollection a thing which, through excess of love for the Lady Bedr-el-Budur, I had forgotten. Thou sayest that thou canst not approach the Sultan without a rich gift. Then, O my mother, if I place in thy hands an offering richer than any King in the world can make to any other, wilt thou carry out my desire?"

Thinking his words were wild as the wind, and that he could produce no such offering, his mother agreed; but, remembering the Slave of the Lamp, and what had already been done in that way, she stipulated with Aladdin that she would carry out his wish only on condition that it required no further invoking of the Efrite. Aladdin assured her on this and asked her to fetch him a china bowl. Wondering greatly she arose, and brought the bowl to him. Then Aladdin emptied into it all the sparkling jewels which he carried within his garments, and, when they were heaped together in the bowl they shone with a dazzling splendor. But, since he realized that it was not impossible that the project might fail, and that he might have to seek to the Slave of the Lamp for advice and help in difficulty, he spoke to his mother on the matter. "O my mother," he said, "it was the condition of thy promise that I should not invoke the Slave of the Lamp in the furtherance of this my desire; yet it must be understood between us that if thou make a blunder—which thou needst not do—then, to extricate us from a dire calamity, I am free to rub the Lamp and see what its Slave can do for our salvation."

His mother assented to this, for she knew, if she failed with the Sultan, all was lost; and, in such case, even the aid of a demon would be acceptable.

When morning dawned Aladdin's mother arose and prepared herself for the visit to the palace, and, wrapping the bowl of jewels in a cloth, went forth early. When the audience was full the Sultan came in and seated himself on the royal divan. All bowed down before him, and then stood waiting with folded arms for his permission to be seated. And, when he gave permission,

all sat down in their due order of precedence. Then he listened to their petitions in the same order, and gave his decisions, until the hour grew late, and the audience was declared closed. The Sultan arose and went into the palace, and the princes, with the nobles and the people, went their ways. Among them went Aladdin's mother, thinking to herself that this would be a matter of many days. And every day thereafter she stood in the audience with the bowl of jewels under her arm and heard the petitions, but dared not for very timidity address the Sultan. And in this way she continued for a whole month, while Aladdin was nursing his impatient soul and waiting on the issue.

Now the Sultan, being observant, had noticed the woman present herself constantly at the levee. So he commanded the Vizier to see to it that, should the woman present herself again, she be instantly brought before him.

And it came according to the Sultan's command to the Grand Vizier; for one day the Sultan saw her waiting in the audience chamber and ordered the Vizier to bring her forward that he might consider her affair.

Now, at last, she was face to face with the Sultan, making obeisance to him and kissing the ground at his feet. "I have seen thee here, O woman, for many days," said the Sultan; "and thou hast not approached me. If thou hast a wish that I can grant, lay it before me." At this she kissed the ground again, and prayed fervently for the prolongation of his life. Then she said, "O King of all the Ages, I have a request; but, peace be on thee, it is a strange one! Wherefore I claim thy clemency before I state it."

These words whetted the Sultan's curiosity, and, as he was a man of great gentleness, he spoke to her softly in reply, and not only assured her of his clemency but ordered all others present to withdraw, saving only the Grand Vizier, so that he might hear her petition in secret.

"Now, woman," said the Sultan, turning to her, "make thy petition, and the peace and protection of God be on thee." "Thy forgiveness, also, O King," she said. "God forgive thee if there is aught to forgive," he replied. And at this

Aladdin's mother unfolded the tale of her son's exceeding love for Bedr-el-Budur, the Sultan's daughter: how life had become intolerable to him because of this, and how his only thought was to win the Lady Bedr-el-Budur for his wife, or die—either of grief, or by the Sultan's anger. Wherefore, his life being in the balance in any case, she had come as a last resort to beg the Sultan to bestow his daughter on her son. And she concluded by beseeching the Sultan not to punish either her or her son for this unparalleled hardihood.

The Sultan looked at the Grand Vizier, whose face was of stone — for the Lady Bedr-el-Budur had already been promised to his son. "What sayest thou?" said the Sultan, regarding him with merriment in his eyes. But the Grand Vizier only cast a contemptuous look at Aladdin's mother, and answered him: "O King of the Age! Thou knowest how to deal with this petition." At this the Sultan laughed outright, and, turning a kindly face to the humble suppliant, observed her minutely. "What is that bundle thou hast under thine arm?" he said at last, remembering that she had brought it with her on every occasion.

Aladdin's mother, greatly relieved to see the Sultan laughing, unfolded the wrappings of the bowl and handed it to him. As soon as he took it in his hand, and saw the size and splendid sparkle of the jewels, the Sultan laughed no longer, but gazed at them, speechless with wonder and admiration. Then at length, he handed the bowl to the Grand Vizier, saying, "Upon my oath, this is a marvellous thing! Tell me, O Vizier, have I in my treasury a single jewel that will compare with even the smallest of these?"

The Grand Vizier also was taken aback by their dazzling loveliness and beauty. He would have lied, saying they were glass or crystal, but the stones themselves flashed back the purposed lie in his teeth. All he could reply was, "Never, O my lord the King, have I beheld the like of these; nor is there one in thy treasury that could equal the beauty of the smallest of them." And, saying this, the Vizier turned very pale, for neither he nor his son could approach the Sultan with such a gift. And it was as he had feared, and as Aladdin had

prophesied: the Sultan required to know nothing further than what was before him in the bowl.

"O Vizier," said the Sultan. "What sayest thou? The man who sends me this kingly gift is worthy of my daughter. I, the Sultan, King of the Age, having power over all men, do withdraw my former promise to thee to bestow her on thy son. Bedr-el-Budur, the one beautiful jewel in the treasury of my heart, is my gift in return to the man who has sent me these priceless jewels."

The Grand Vizier bit his lips and pondered awhile. Then he spoke. "Peace be on thee, O King of all the Earth. But is not thy promise worth most of all? Thou didst pledge me thy daughter for my son, and with that pledge I went, thinking that the whole earth and all therein were not its value. Wherefore, O King, I pray that thou wilt allow this matter time. If thou wilt pledge this foster-mother of a prince that thou wilt comply with her request in three months' time, then it seems to me that, by so doing, thou wilt cement the good feeling and loosen the griefs of all parties concerned. And in the meantime—yea, I have good reason for saying it—there will come before thee, O King of the Age, a gift compared to which this thou hast seen is but dross."

The Sultan weighed the Grand Vizier's words in his mind, and accordingly, he said to the woman, "Tell thy son that he hath my royal assent, and that I will give him my daughter in marriage; but, as every woman knows, these things cannot be hastened, for there are garments and necessaries to be prepared; wherefore thy son (on whom be peace) must abide in patience, for, let us say, three months. At the end of that time he may approach me for the fulfillment of my promise."

Satisfied with this, Aladdin's mother thanked and blessed the Sultan, and, buoyed up with delight, almost flew back to her house. There Aladdin was waiting for her, and, when he saw her hastening, and noticed that she had returned without the bowl of jewels, his heart rose high to meet her.

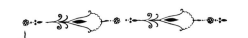 

Then she related to him the details of the interview, laying stress upon the fact that, although the Sultan had been moved at the sight of the jewels to make immediate arrangements for the marriage, a private word from the Grand Vizier had led him to delay the ceremony for three months. "Take heed, my son!" she concluded. "The Grand Vizier hath a motive for this counsel of delay. He is thine enemy. I saw it in his face. Beware of him!"

Aladdin was greatly relieved by her news. He felt like one jerked out of the grave; and, where the Sultan was favorable to his suit, he was in no mood to fear a Grand Vizier. "Nay, nay," he said, "the jewels have the eye of the Sultan more than the Grand Vizier hath his ear. Fear nothing, O my mother! The Sultan's word is good, and I rest content to wait; though I know not how such a long time as three months can be got into the calendar."

Two of these long, weary months went by, and Aladdin nursed his soul in patience. Then a thing happened which gave him seriously to think. On a day in the first week of the third month his mother went forth into the market place about sunset to buy oil, and she saw that all the shops were closed, and the people were adorning their windows with bright garlands as if for some festivity. She wondered greatly at this, thinking the Sultan had either changed his birthday or that another child had been born to him. Yet she had gleaned nothing of any great event from the gossip of her neighbors. Having, after much difficulty, found an oil shop open, she bought her oil, and questioned the man. "Uncle," she said; "what is abroad in the city that the people close their shops and place candles and garlands in their windows?" "Thou art evidently a stranger," replied the man. "Nay, I am of this city," said she. "Then must thou cleanse thine ears," he retorted. "Hast thou not heard that the Grand Vizier's son is to take to himself this evening the beautiful Bedr-el-Budur? Surely, woman, thou hast been sleeping all day on thine ears, for the news went abroad early this morning. The Vizier's son is at the Hammam, and these soldiers and officials you see in the streets are waiting to escort him to the palace. And, you are fortunate to get oil today, for all those

 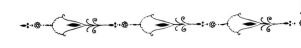

who purvey oil to the Grand Vizier and his household have closed their shops as a mark of respect."

Aladdin's mother went home in a state of great consternation. Though her feet hastened, her heart lagged behind her, for she knew not how to tell her son the terrible news. She was afraid that after his joy at the Sultan's promise, and his patient waiting, this blow would send him out of his mind. Then she contrived it in her thoughts that it was best to provoke her son's anger against the Sultan, rather than his grief at the loss of Bedr-el-Budur. Accordingly, as soon as she entered the house and found him sitting thinking, as was his wont of late, she said, "O my son, there is no faith nor trust but in God. Said I not to thee that the Grand Vizier was thine enemy? Out on him and the Sultan, for their word is but hot wind, and there is no faith in the promise of a King." "I see by thy face and by thy speech," said Aladdin, "that thou hast some bad news. What is it, O my mother?"

Then his mother told how the Sultan had violated his covenant, and how the marriage of the Lady Bedr-el-Budur to the Grand Vizier's son was to take place that very evening. For this she heaped abuse upon the Grand Vizier, saying that it was only the worst of men that could so lead the Sultan to break his promise. When she had told all, and Aladdin understood how the matter lay, he arose, more in anger than in grief, and cried out against the Grand Vizier and cursed all the parties concerned in the affair. But presently he remembered that, when all seemed lost, he still had the Lamp, and that was something in time of trouble and difficulty.

With this he arose and retired to his own chamber, where he brought out the Lamp. Then, having considered well the manner of his wish, he rubbed it. Immediately the Efrite stepped out of the unseen and stood before him, saying, "Thou hast invoked me: what is thy desire? I am the Slave of the Lamp in thy hand and am here to do thy bidding." And Aladdin answered: "Know, O Slave of the Lamp, that the Sultan promised me his daughter for my wife, but he has broken his word, and this night she is to be united with

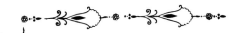 

the Grand Vizier's son; wherefore I wish that, as soon as the pair retire, thou take them up, with the couch whereon they lie, and bring them hither to me." "I hear and obey," said the Slave of the Lamp, and immediately vanished.

Aladdin waited expectantly for some time, for he guessed that the moment would not be long delayed when the wedded pair would retire from the ceremonies. And his guess was right, for when he had waited a little longer, suddenly a cold blast of air swept through the chamber; the wall opened and there appeared the Efrite bearing in his arms the wedded pair upon the nuptial couch. They had been transported in the twinkling of an eye, and when the Efrite had set the couch down at Aladdin's feet, they were both stupefied with astonishment at this proceeding.

"Take that scurvy thief," said Aladdin to the Efrite, pointing to the Vizier's son, "and bind him and lodge him in the wood-closet for the night." And the Efrite did so. He took up the Vizier's son in one hand, and, reaching with the other for cords, drew them from the invisible and bound the miscreant securely. Then he placed him in the wood-closet and blew an icy blast upon him to comfort him. Returning to Aladdin he said, "It is done, O Master of the Lamp! Is there aught else thou dost desire?" "Naught but this," replied Aladdin. "In the morning, when the Sultan is proceeding towards their chamber to wish them long life and happiness, convey them back thither in a state of sleep so that the Sultan's knock at their door may wake them." "I will obey," said the Efrite, and, in a moment, the air closed over him and he was gone.

And Aladdin smiled to himself to think that this thing had been done. Then he turned to the Lady Bedr-el-Budur, who was sitting weeping on the couch. "O lovely one," said he, "weep not; for I would not hurt one hair of thy head, nor sully thine honor in any way. Know that I love thee too much to harm thee; but, since thy father the Sultan promised me thee, and has violated his word, I am determined that none other shall call thee his. Rest in

The Lady Bedr-el-Budur

peace, lovely lady; for neither am I thy husband nor the thief of thy husband's honor. Wherefore, weep not, but rest in peace."

So saying he took a sword that hung on the wall of his chamber, and, having placed it by her side in token of security, he stretched himself upon the couch so that they lay with the sword between them. Thus they passed the night. The Sultan's daughter wept the long night through, and Aladdin could not close his eyes for thinking of his unfortunate rival's condition in the wood-closet. Towards morning Bedr-el-Budur, utterly exhausted with weeping, fell asleep; and, as Aladdin gazed upon her, he saw that indeed her loveliness was rare; and, the more he gazed, the more he thought of the unhappy fate of the Vizier's son. Never was a man so badly treated as to be bound fast on his wedding night and laid in a wood-closet in deadly fear of the dreadful apparition that had placed him there.

In the morning, while Bedr-el-Budur still slept, the Slave of the Lamp appeared according to Aladdin's command. "O my master," he said, "the Sultan hath left his couch and is about to knock at the door of the bridal chamber. I am here to perform thy bidding on the instant." "So be it," answered Aladdin. "Convey them together on the couch back to their place." And scarcely had he spoken when the Efrite vanished and reappeared with the Vizier's son, whom he quickly unbound and laid upon the couch beside the sleeping Bedr-el-Budur. Then, lifting the couch with the two upon it, he vanished, and Aladdin knew that, before the Sultan had knocked at the door of the bridal chamber, everything would be as it had been. Everything? No, not everything; for the Lady Bedr-el-Budur must awake as from a terrible nightmare; and, as for the Vizier's son, would he sing a song to the Sultan about spending the night in the wood-closet? Aladdin pondered over this and decided that nothing less than a repetition of the affair would wring the truth from either of them.

At this moment the Sultan knocked at the door of the bridal chamber in the palace, and the Vizier's son, still cold from the wood-closet, arose and

opened to him. The Sultan advanced to the couch, and kissed his daughter, and asked her if she was happy and content. By way of answer she glared at him in sullen silence, for she had not forgotten, in dreams or in waking, what had happened to her. The Sultan, not understanding what had befallen, and feeling annoyed, turned and left the chamber to lay the matter before the Queen, to whose ear their daughter's tongue might the more easily be loosed. So he came to the Queen and told her how Bedr-el-Budur had received him, concluding his recital with the remark, "Thus it is; there is trouble behind the door of that bridal chamber."

But the Queen smiled at his serious fears and answered him: "O my lord the King, thou knowest little of the heart of a woman. When it is happiest, a trifle makes it sad; and, when it would send tears of laughter and joy to the eyes, it sometimes turns perverse against itself for very gladness, and sends tears of pain instead. Wherefore, be not angry with her, but let me go and see her. She will surely confide in me."

So saying, she arose and robed herself, and went to the bridal chamber. At first sight of her daughter's dejected attitude and pained expression she imagined that some lovers' quarrel over a mere trifle had occurred; but when she kissed her, wishing her good morning, and Bedr-el-Budur answered no word to her salutation, she began to think that some grave trouble rested on her daughter's mind. And it was not until she had coaxed her, and used every argument known to a mother, that she received an answer to her questions. "Be not angry with me, O my mother," said Bedr-el-Budur at last, raising her sad beautiful eyes, "but know that a terrible thing has happened—a thing which I hardly dare tell thee lest thou think I have lost my reason. Scarcely had we retired, O my mother, when there suddenly appeared a huge black shape—terrible, horrific in aspect; and this—I know not what nor who—lifted the couch whereon we lay and conveyed us in a flash to some dark and vile abode of the common people." And then to her mother's astonished ears she unfolded the tale of all that had happened during the

night till, suddenly, in the morning, she awoke to find the monstrous shape replacing them in the bridal chamber at the moment her father the Sultan had knocked at the door. "And that, O my mother," she concluded, "is why I could not answer my father, for I was so bewildered and stricken with unhappiness that I thought that I was mad; though, now I have thought about the affair from beginning to end, I know that I have my wits like any other."

"Truly, O my daughter," said the Queen with great concern, "if thou were to tell this story to thy father he would say thou wert mad. Wherefore, I counsel thee, child, tell it to him not; neither to him nor to any other one." "Nay, O my mother," answered Bedr-el-Budur, "dost thou doubt it, ask my husband if my tale be true or not." But the Queen replied, "Sweep these fancies from thy mind, O my daughter; and arise and robe thyself to attend the rejoicings which this day have been prepared in the city in thine honor. For the people are in glad array, and the drums will beat and music will delight the ears of all; and the musicians will sing thy praises and all will wish thee long life and happiness."

Leaving Bedr-el-Budur, then, with her tirewomen, the Queen sought the Sultan, and begged him not to be angry with their daughter, for she had been distressed with unhappy dreams. Then she sent for the Vizier's son to come to her secretly, and, when he stood before her, she related to him what Bedr-el-Budur had told her, and asked him if it were true or if he knew aught of it. "Nay," he answered, for he had thought the matter over and feared that the truth might rob him of his bride; besides, his acquaintance with the wood-closet seemed to him discreditable, and he felt little inclined to boast of it. "Nay, O my lady the Queen," said he; "I know naught of these things beyond what thou hast told me."

From this there was no doubt left in the Queen's mind that her daughter had suffered from a nightmare so vivid that she had been unable easily to cast it from her. Nevertheless, she felt assured that, as the day wore on, with its

gaieties and rejoicings, Bedr-el-Budur would be enabled to rid herself of these troubled imaginings of the night, and resume her former self.

At eventime, when the wild rejoicing of the city had fatigued itself against replenishment by wine, Aladdin retired to his chamber and rubbed the Lamp. Immediately the Slave appeared and desired to know his wish. "O Slave of the Lamp," said Aladdin, "do as thou didst last night. See to it that thou convey the bridal pair hither again as man and maid at the eleventh hour of their innocence." The Slave of the Lamp vanished in a moment, and Aladdin sat for a long time; yet he was content, for he knew that the wily Efrite was but awaiting his opportunity. At length the monster reappeared before him, bearing in his arms the bridal couch with the pair upon it, weeping and wringing their hands in excess of grief and terror. And, at Aladdin's word the Slave took the Vizier's son as before and put him to bed in the wood-closet, where he remained, bound fast in an icy chill. And when it was morning, and the Sultan was about to knock at the door of the bridal chamber in the palace, the Slave of the Lamp appeared and conveyed the bride and the bridegroom swiftly back to their place.

The Sultan had come to wish his daughter good morning, and to see also if she would behave towards him as on the former occasion.

Then Bedr-el-Budur wept and supplicated him, and told him what had befallen on the second night as on the first.

The Sultan repaired immediately to the Grand Vizier and told him all; and asked him whether he had received the same version of this matter from his son. But the Grand Vizier shook his head in the manner of one who might be lying and might not. "Then," said the Sultan, "go at once and question him, for it may be that my daughter hath seen visions and dreamed dreams; although, I am unable to disbelieve the truth of her story."

So the Grand Vizier went and inquired of his son, and presently returned to the Sultan in great perplexity of face, for his son, whatever he had admitted before, had now confessed to everything, even to the wood-closet.

And, moreover he had begged and implored his father to obtain his release from this most unhappy marriage, since it was better to be without a bride and sleep in peace than to have one and perish with cold in a wood-closet. Thus it was with the Vizier's son.

"O King of the Age," said the Grand Vizier, who could not see his way to conceal the truth, "my son telleth the same tale as thy daughter, the Lady Bedr-el-Budur. Wherefore I beseech thee that thou set a guard this night, so that —" "Nay," broke in the Sultan angrily; "it is an unhappy marriage and bodes no good. Thou didst persuade me that my promise to that woman in respect of her son was not binding, but these unhappy events and ill-omened affairs make me think thou wast mistaken. Abide not another night, for worse may happen. Go forth, O Vizier, and proclaim the marriage annulled. Bid the people cease to rejoice, and command all to go their own ways and behave as if the marriage had not been."

At this the Grand Vizier bowed his head and went forth exceedingly angry, and proclaimed the annulment of the marriage to all the people.

Whether the Sultan had swiftly forgotten or tardily remembered his pledge, Aladdin troubled not to inquire. He waited patiently until the three months had expired, and then sent his mother to demand of the Sultan the fulfillment of his promise.

The Sultan, who had not now the bowl of jewels before him to blind his vision, regarded her intently, and saw that she was of humble state. "What is thy thought on this, O Vizier?" he said. "My word is my word, and I regret that thou shouldst have explained it away; yet it seems to me that this woman is not of the kind that could mother-in-law my daughter. Hast thou a plan which is not a trick? If thou hast, whisper it in my ear."

The Grand Vizier was pleased to hear the Sultan appealing to his ready wit in this way. "O King of the Age," he said, "thy pledge holds good, as ever it did; yea, as good as marriage vows. But verily, if this common woman's son desireth thy daughter for his wife, there should be a settlement befitting

such a suit. Wherefore ask of him forty bowls of gold filled with jewels of the same blood and tincture as the woman brought at first, with forty female slaves to carry them, and a fitting retinue of forty. This thing, which is a Sultan's right to ask, it seemeth to me he cannot contrive to execute, and thus thou shalt be free of him."

"By Allah!" said the Sultan, "thou art of ready wit, O Vizier! Truly a marriage settlement is needed." Then, turning to Aladdin's mother, he said: "O woman! know that when one asketh the daughter of the Sultan one must have standing, for so it is in royal circles; and, to prove that standing, the suitor must show that he is able to provide for the Sultan's daughter and keep her in that state to which she has been accustomed. Wherefore he must bring to me forty golden bowls filled with jewels such as thou didst bring, with forty beautiful female slaves to carry them and forty black slaves as a retinue. Coming like this, thy son may claim my daughter, for the Sultan's word is the Sultan's word."

A sad woman then was Aladdin's mother. She returned to her son sick at heart. "O my son," she exclaimed, weeping, "said I not to thee that the Grand Vizier was thine enemy? The Sultan remembered his pledge, but the Vizier—may his bones rot!—whispered in his ear, and the outcome is this: forty golden bowls of jewels, forty female slaves to carry them, and forty slaves as an escort. With this dowry, O my son, thou mayest approach the Sultan and claim his daughter as thy bride."

Loudly Aladdin laughed to scorn. And when his mother had brought him food, and he had eaten, he arose and went into his chamber. There he brought out the Lamp, and, sitting down, he rubbed it. Immediately the Slave appeared.

In less than an hour he returned and led before Aladdin forty beautiful maidens, each carrying a golden bowl of jewels on her head, and each accompanied by a magnificent black slave. And when Aladdin's mother saw this array she knew that it was done by the Lamp, and she blessed it for her

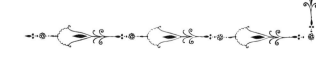

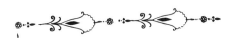 

son's sake. Then said Aladdin, "O my mother, behold, the dowry is ready according to the Sultan's requirement. It is for thee to take it to him, to show him what is in my power, and also that no time hath been lost in complying with his request."

Then the maids, with the golden bowls of precious stones, arrayed themselves in the street outside the house, and by each maid stood a slave. Thus, led by Aladdin's mother, they proceeded to the Sultan's palace; and the people crowded in the streets to see this unwonted sight, for the maids were richly dressed, and all, with the sun shining on their raiment and flashing in the jewels they bore, made a magnificent spectacle. Never had the people seen such jewels, never such beauteous damsels, never such magnificent slaves.

Thus, in due course, came Aladdin's mother before the Sultan, leading the cortège into the Audience Hall. The maidens took the bowls of jewels from their heads and set them on the ground. Then they made obeisance, they and the slaves prostrating themselves before the Sultan; and, having done this, they all arose and stood before him in humble reverence. And, when the Sultan's gaze at last left the beauteous damsels and fell upon the bowls of jewels at their feet, he was beside himself with wonder and admiration. When he found words, he commanded that the whole cortège should present itself, with the jewels, to the Lady Bedr-el-Budur in her palace. Then he added to Aladdin's mother: "Tell thy son he need fear not but that I shall keep my promise; but bid him come hither to me with all haste, so that I may look upon his face and accept him as my son-in-law; for the marriage shall be this very night."

The Grand Vizier turned white with rage — whiter than his false heart had ever been, even when a boy. After a dagger-thrust of glances between them, Aladdin's mother made obeisance to the Sultan and thanked him. Then, with contempt for the Grand Vizier written plainly on her face, she withdrew, and returned home, walking on air.

Now Aladdin, when he saw his mother returning swift-footed and on wings of joy, knew that good tidings came with her. But, before he could speak, his mother burst in upon him and embraced him, crying, "O my son! thy heart's wish is fulfilled. This very night thou art to wed the Sultan's daughter, and so it is proclaimed before all the world." Then did Aladdin rejoice that his expectations were fulfilled, and was continuing to rejoice when his mother addressed him suddenly. "Nay," she said, "I have not told thee all. The Sultan bids thee go to him immediately, for he desires to see his son-in-law. But how shalt thou approach the Sultan in thy merchant's garments? However, I have done all I can for thee, and it is now thine own affair."

So saying, she withdrew to rest a little, and Aladdin, having blessed her, retired to his chamber and brought forth the Lamp. With a set purpose in his mind, he rubbed it, and at once the Slave appeared. "Thou knowest me: what is thy desire?" "I wish," answered Aladdin, "that thou take me to a bath which hath no equal in all the kingdoms, and provide me there with a change of raiment of resplendent glory, richer than any the Sultan has ever worn."

No sooner had he spoken than the Efrite bore him away in his arms, and deposited him in a bath the like of which no King could compass nor any man describe. Then he sought the jewelled hall and found there, in place of his merchant's garb, a set of robes that exceeded all imagination. At the door of the bath, he was met by the Efrite in waiting, who took up and bore him in a flash to his home.

"Hast thou still some further need?" asked the Slave of the Lamp, about to vanish. "Yea," replied Aladdin. "Bring me here a Chief of Memluks with forty-eight in his train — twenty-four to precede me and twenty-four to follow after; and see that they have splendid horses and equipments, so that not even the greatest in the world can say, 'This is inferior to mine.' For myself I want a stallion such as cannot be equalled among the Arabs, and his housings must be for value such as one could purchase only in dreams. And to each

memluk give a thousand gold pieces, and the the Chief Memluk ten thousand; for we go to the Sultan's palace and would scatter largesse on the way. Wait! Also twelve maidens of unequalled grace and loveliness in person to attire and accompany my mother to the Sultan's presence. And look you! whatever of grace and beauty is lacking in my person supply it to me on my natural plan of being. See to it, O Slave of the Lamp!"

"It is already done," said the Slave of the Lamp; and, vanishing on the instant, he reappeared at once at the doorway of the house, leading a noble white stallion gorgeously equipped, while behind came the twelve damsels and forty-nine memluks on magnificent chargers.

Now, when the Sultan had received word that Aladdin was coming, he informed his nobles and grandees of the meaning of this thing; so that, when Aladdin arrived, there was a vast concourse of people, and all the stateliest of the land were there awaiting his entry. As the sun rises in glory upon a waiting world, so came Aladdin to the palace. At the door of the Hall of Audience he dismounted, while hands held his stirrup that had never performed such an office before.

The Sultan was seated on his throne, and, immediately when he saw Aladdin, he arose and descended and took him to his breast, forbidding all ceremony on so great an occasion. Then he led him up affectionately, and placed him on his right hand. In all this Aladdin forgot not the respect due to kings. Forbidden to be too humble, he was not too lofty in his bearing. He spoke:

"O my lord the Sultan! King of the Earth and Heaven's Dispenser of all Good! Truly thou hast treated me graciously in bestowing upon me thy daughter the Lady Bedr-el-Budur. Hear me yet further, for I have a request to make. Grant me a site whereon to build a palace, unworthy as it may prove, for the comfort and happiness of thy daughter, the Lady Bedr-el-Budur!"

Then the Sultan conversed with Aladdin and was greatly charmed with his courtliness and eloquence. Anon he ordered the musicians to play, and

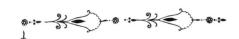

together they listened to the music in the utmost content. Finally he arose, and, taking Aladdin by the hand, led him forth into the palace banqueting hall, where a splendid supper was awaiting them with the lords of the land standing ready in their proper order of degree. Yet above them all sat Aladdin, for he was at the Sultan's right hand. And, while they ate, the music played and a merry wit prevailed; and the Sultan drew nearer to Aladdin in their talk, and saw, from his grace, his manner of speech, and his complaisance, that indeed he must have been brought up and nurtured among kings. Then, while they conversed, the Sultan's heart went out with joy and satisfaction to Aladdin, and the whole assemblage saw that it was not as it had been with the Vizier's son.

The Grand Vizier himself would have retired early had it not been that his presence was required for the marriage ceremony. As soon as the banquet was over and the tables cleared away, the Sultan commanded the Vizier to summon the Kadis and the witnesses, and thus the contract between Aladdin and the Lady Bedr-el-Budur was duly executed. Then, without a warning word, Aladdin arose to depart. "Wherefore, O my son?" said the Sultan. "Thy wedding is duly contracted and the festivities are about to begin."

"Yea, O my lord the King," replied Aladdin; "and none rejoiceth at that more than I; but, if it please thee, it is my thought to build a palace for the Lady Bedr-el-Budur; and if my love and longing for her be anything, thou mayest rest assured that it will be completed so quickly as to amaze thee." At this the Grand Vizier tugged the Sultan's sleeve, but received no attention. "It is well," said the Sultan to Aladdin; "choose what site seemeth best to thee and follow thine own heart in the matter. See this open space by my palace! What thinkest thou, my son?" "O King," replied Aladdin, "I cannot thank thee enough, for it is the summit of my felicity to be near thee."

Then Aladdin left the palace in the same royal manner as he had approached it, with his memluks preceding and following; and again the people praised and blessed him as he passed. When he reached his house

he left all other affairs in the hands of his Chief Memluk with certain instructions, and went into his chamber. There he took the Lamp and rubbed it. The Slave appeared on the instant and desired to know his pleasure. "O Slave," answered Aladdin, "I have a great task for thee. I desire thee to build for me in all haste a palace on the open space near the Sultan's serai—a palace of magnificent design and construction, and filled with rare and costly things. And let it be incomplete in one small respect, so that, when the Sultan offers to complete it to match the whole, all the wealth and artifice at his command will not suffice for the task." "O my master," replied the Efrite, "it shall be done with all speed. I will return when the work is finished." With this he vanished.

It was an hour before dawn when the Slave of the Lamp returned to Aladdin, and, awakening him from sleep, stood before him. "O Master of the Lamp," he said, "the palace is built as thou didst command." "It is well, O Slave of the Lamp," answered Aladdin; "and I would inspect thy work." No sooner had he spoken than he found himself being borne swiftly through the air in the arms of the Efrite, who set him down almost immediately within the palace.

Most excellently had the Slave done his work. Porphyry, jasper, alabaster and other rare stones had been used in the construction of the building. The floors were of mosaics which to match would cost much wealth and time in the fashioning, while the walls and ceilings, the doors and the smallest pieces of detail were all such that even the imagining of them could come only to one dissatisfied with the palaces of kings. When Aladdin had wondered at all this, the Slave led him into the Treasury, and showed him countless bars of gold and silver and gems of dazzling brilliance. Thence to the banqueting hall, where the tables were arrayed in a manner to take one's breath away; for every dish and every flagon was of gold or silver, and all the goblets were crusted with jewels. But, when the Slave led him farther and showed him a pavilion with twenty-four niches thickly set with diamonds and emeralds and

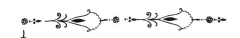

Aladdin and the Magic Lamp

rubies, he fairly lost his wits. And the Slave took him to one niche and showed him how his command had been carried out in that this was the one small part of the palace that was left incomplete in order to tempt and tax the Sultan to finish it.

When Aladdin had viewed the whole palace, and seen the numerous slaves and beautiful maidens therein, he asked yet one thing more of the Efrite. "O Slave of the Lamp," he said, "the work is wonderful, yet it still lacketh an approach from the Sultan's palace. I desire, therefore, a rich carpet laid upon the intervening space, so that the Lady Bedr-el-Budur may come and go upon a splendid pathway of brocade worked with gold and inlaid with precious stones." "I hear and obey," said the Slave, and vanished. Presently he returned and led Aladdin to the steps of the palace. "O my lord," he said, "what thou didst command is done." And he pointed to a magnificent carpet extending from palace to palace. The gold and the precious stones in the brocade gleamed and sparkled in the stars' last rays before the rise of dawn. When Aladdin had gazed upon it and wondered at it, the Efrite carried him in the twinkling of an eye back to his own home.

Shortly afterwards, when the dawn had arisen, the Sultan opened his eyes, and, looking forth from his window, beheld a magnificent structure where the day before had been an open space. Doubting the evidence of his senses, he turned himself about and rubbed his eyes and looked again. There, undoubtedly, was a palace more splendid and glorious than any he had ever seen; and there, leading to it, was a carpet the like of which he had never trod. The news of it spread through the palace like wildfire. The Grand Vizier came rushing to the Sultan, and, finding him at the window, had no need to tell him the cause of his excitement. "What sayest thou, O Vizier?" said the Sultan. "Yonder stands a palace surpassing all others. Truly Aladdin is worthy of my daughter, since at his bidding such a royal edifice arises in a single night."

154

Then the Vizier's envy found vent. "O King," he said, "thinkest thou that such a thing as this could be done save by the vilest of sorcery? Riches and jewels and costly attire are in the hands of mortals, but this—this is impossible!" "Impossible?" said the Sultan. "Behold!—and he pointed towards the palace—"there it stands in the light of day, and thou sayest it is impossible. Verily, O Vizier, it seems thy wits are turned with envy at the wealth of Aladdin. Prate not to me of sorcery. There are few things beyond the power of a man in whose treasury are such jewels as those sent me by Aladdin." At this the Grand Vizier was silent; indeed, his excess of envy well night choked him, for he saw that the Sultan loved Aladdin greatly.

Now when Aladdin awoke in the morning and knew that he must set forth for the palace where the nobles and grandees were already assembling for the wedding celebration, he took the Lamp and rubbed it. The Slave appeared on the instant and desired to know his wish. "O Slave of the Lamp," said Aladdin, "this is my wedding day and I go to the Sultan's palace. Wherefore I shall need ten thousand gold pieces."

When all was ready Aladdin mounted his steed and rode through the city while the memluks before and behind distributed largesse all the way. And the people were loud in their praises of his dignity and grace and loved him greatly for his generosity. Anon the palace was reached and there the high officials, who were looking for Aladdin and his train, hastened to inform the Sultan of his approach. On this the Sultan arose, and, going out to the gates of the palace to meet him, embraced and kissed him.

Anon the Sultan commanded the wedding banquet to be served. And, when it was all ready, Aladdin sat on the right hand of the Sultan; and they, with all the nobles and foremost in the land, ate and drank. On every hand were honor and good will for Aladdin.

When the banquet was over Aladdin repaired with his memluks to his palace to make ready for the reception of his bride, Bedr-el-Budur. And, as he went, all the people thronged him, shouting, "God give thee happiness! God bless thy days!" And he scattered gold amongst them.

Bedr-el-Budur, watching him from a window in her father's palace, felt her heart turn over and over in her bosom, and then, saying within herself, "He is my husband and none other," she renounced herself to the exquisite joy of sudden love.

At eventime the Sultan commanded an escort to conduct the Lady Bedr-el-Budur to her husband's abode. On this the Captains of guards, the officers of state and nobles, well equipped, were mounted in readiness and waiting at the door of Bedr-el-Budur's apartments. Presently, preceded by female slaves and eunuchs bearing lighted tapers set in jewelled candlesticks, came forth a vision of loveliness. Bedr-el-Budur, aflame with love for Aladdin, appeared on the threshold like a pure white bird about to fly into space. All too slow was the procession that escorted her to Aladdin's palace. The stately pomp and splendor accorded not with the beating of her heart. She saw not Aladdin's mother nor the beauteous damsels, nor the mounted guards, nor the emirs, nor the nobles — her only thought was Aladdin, for her heart was consumed with love.

Thus from the Seraglio to Aladdin's palace, where Bedr-el-Budur, as one floating in a dream, was taken to her apartments and arrayed for presentation to the Court assembled. And of all that Court and multitude of people the only one who had no voice was Aladdin, for, when he looked upon his bride in her surpassing loveliness, he was reft of speech or thought, and stood silent before a joy too great for tongue to tell.

Great was the Sultan's wonder and admiration when he saw the architecture and masonry of the structure, for, even without, it was all of the rarest and most costly stone inlaid with gold and silver and fashioned with consummate skill; but when he entered and viewed the entrance hall his

breath was snatched away from him, for he had never seen anything so magnificent in his life. At length, finding speech, he turned to the Grand Vizier and said, "Verily, this is the greatest wonder of all. Hast thou ever, from first to last, beheld a palace like this?" "O King of the Age," replied the Vizier gravely, "there hath never been the like of this among the sons of men. It would take ten thousand workmen ten thousand days to construct it; wherefore, as I told thy Felicity, its completion in a single night is the work of sorcery." At this the Sultan was not pleased. "Verily, O Vizier," he replied, "thou hast an envious heart, and thou speakest foolishly with thy mouth."

At this moment Aladdin approached the Sultan to conduct him through the rooms of the palace and, as they went from one to another, the Sultan was simply astounded at the wealth of metal and precious stones on every hand, and at the workmanship thereof. As for the Vizier, he had said all he had to say, and followed sullenly, nursing an evil heart. At length they came to the kiosk, which was a crowning work of jewel-clusters so rich and splendid that the Treasuries of the earth must have been emptied to fill them. The Sultan nearly lost his wits in the effort to calculate the fabulous wealth of this apartment alone. For relief he turned this way and that, gazing upon the niches, which were the most precious and wonderful of all. And in this way he came at length to the niche that had been left incomplete. This gave him speech. "Alas!" he said, relieved to find a flaw, "this niche, at least, is imperfect." Then, turning to Aladdin, he inquired the reason of it. "Yea, O my lord," answered Aladdin, "woe unto it; it is indeed unfinished, for the workmen clamored to be allowed to prepare themselves for the wedding festivities and I had not the heart to say them nay. So they left it as thou seest it." Then, while Aladdin stood by observing intently the effect of his words, the Sultan stroked his beard in contemplation. "O my son," he said presently, "the thought has come to me to complete it myself." "On the head and eye, O King!" cried Aladdin. "And may thy life be prolonged! if thou wilt honor me thus it will be a fitting perpetuation of thy memory in the palace of thy

daughter." At this, the Sultan, vastly pleased, summoned his jewellers and artificers, and, empowering them to draw on the Royal Treasury for all they might require, he commanded them to complete the niche.

Scarcely had the Sultan finished his directions in this matter when Bedr-el-Budur came to greet him. And his heart leapt with joy at her radiant face when he looked upon her. Then, when she had confided to him how happy she was, Aladdin led them into the banqueting hall, where all was ready.

When the Sultan's soul was well nigh weary with excess of enjoyment he rose, and, bethinking himself of the unfinished niche, repaired to the kiosk to see how his workmen had progressed with their task. And when he came to them and inspected their work he saw that they had completed only a small portion and that neither the execution nor the material, which was already exhausted, could compare with that of the other niches. Seeing this he bethought him of his reserve Treasury and the jewels Aladdin had given him. Wherefore he commanded the workmen to draw upon these and continue their work. This they did, and, in due course, the Sultan returned to find that the work was still incomplete. Determined to carry out his design at whatever cost the Sultan commanded his officials to seize all the jewels they could lay their hands on in the kingdom. Even this was done, and lo, still the niche was unfinished.

It was not until late on a day thereafter that Aladdin found the jewellers and goldsmiths adding to the work the last stones at their command. "Hast thou jewels enough?" he asked of the chief artificer. "Nay, O my master," he replied sadly. "We have used all the jewels in the Treasuries; yea, even in all the kingdom, and yet the work is only half finished."

"Take it all away!" said Aladdin. "Restore the jewels to their rightful owners." So they undid their work and returned the jewels to the Treasuries and to the people from whom they had been taken. And they went in to the Sultan and told him. Unable to learn from them the exact reason for this, the Sultan immediately called for his attendants and his horses and repaired to Aladdin's palace.

Meanwhile, Aladdin himself, as soon as the workmen had left, retired to a private chamber; and, taking out the Lamp, rubbed it. "Ask what thou wilt," said the Slave, appearing on the instant. "I desire thee to complete the niche which was left incomplete," answered Aladdin. "I hear and obey," said the Slave, and vanished. In a very short space of time he returned, saying, "O my master, the work is complete." Then Aladdin arose and went to the kiosk, and found that the Slave had spoken truly; the niche was finished. As he was examining it, a memluk came to him and informed him that the Sultan was at the gates. At this Aladdin hastened to meet him. "O my son," cried the Sultan as Aladdin greeted him, "why didst thou not let my jewellers complete the niche in the kiosk? Wilt thou not have the palace whole?" And Aladdin answered him, "O my lord, I left it unfinished in order to raise a doubt in thy mind and then dispel it; for, if thy Felicity doubted my ability to finish it, a glance at the kiosk as it now stands will make the matter plain." And he led the Sultan to the kiosk and showed him the completed niche.

The Sultan's astonishment was now greater than ever, that Aladdin had accomplished in so short a space that which he himself could command neither workmen nor jewels sufficient to accomplish in many months. It filled him with wonder. He embraced Aladdin and kissed him, saying there was none like him in all the world. Then, when he had rested awhile with his daughter Bedr-el-Budur, who was full of joy and happiness, the Sultan returned to his own palace.

As the days passed by Aladdin's fame went forth through all the land.

Now it chanced that the Sultan's enemies from distant parts invaded his territory and rode down against him. The Sultan assembled his armies for war and gave the chief command to Aladdin, whose skill and prowess had found great favor in his eyes. And Bedr-el-Budur wept when Aladdin went forth to the wars, but great was her delight when he returned victorious, having routed the enemy in a great battle with terrible slaughter.

Now the fame of Aladdin penetrated even to distant parts, so that his name was heard even in the land of the Moors, where the accursed Dervish dwelt. This sorcerer had not yet made an end of lamenting the loss of the Lamp just as it seemed about to pass into his hands. And, while he lamented, he cursed Aladdin in his bitter rage, saying within himself. "'Tis well that ill-omened miscreant is dead and buried, for, if I have not the Lamp, it is at least safe, and one day I may come by it." But when he heard the name "Aladdin," and the fame attached to it, he muttered to himself, "Can this be he? And hath he risen to a high position through the Lamp and the Slave of the Lamp?" Then he rose and drew a table of magic signs in the sand in order to find if the Aladdin of Destiny were indeed alive upon the earth. And the figures gave him what he feared. Aladdin was alive and the Lamp was not in the cavern where by his magic he had first discovered it. At this a great fear struck him to the heart, and he wondered that he had lived to experience it, for he knew that at any moment Aladdin, by means of the Slave of the Lamp, might slay him for revenge. Wondering that this had not occurred to Aladdin's mind he hastened to draw another table; by which he saw that Aladdin had acquired great possessions and had married the Sultan's daughter. At this his rage mastered his fear and he cursed Aladdin with fury and envy. But, though his magic was great, it could not cope with that which slumbered in the Lamp, and his curses missed their mark, only to abide the time when they might circle back upon him. Meanwhile, in great haste, he arose and journeyed to the far land of Cathay, fearing every moment that Aladdin would bethink him of revenge by means of the Slave of the Lamp. Yet he arrived safely at the City of the Sultan and rested at an inn where he heard naught but praises of Aladdin's generosity, his bravery in battle, his beautiful bride Bedr-el-Budur and his magnificent palace.

Taking his instruments of divination, he soon learned that the Lamp was not on Aladdin's person, but in the palace. At this he was overjoyed, for he had a plan to get possession of it. Then he went out into the market and

bought a great number of new lamps, which he put in a basket and took back to the inn. When evening was drawing nigh, he took the basket and went forth in the city — for such was his plan — crying, "New lamps for old! Who will exchange old lamps for new?" And the people hearing this, laughed among themselves, saying he was mad; and none brought an old lamp to him in exchange for a new one, for they all thought there was nothing to be gained out of a madman. But when the Dervish reached Aladdin's palace he began to cry more lustily, "New lamps for old! Who will exchange old lamps for new?" And he took no heed of the boys who mocked him and the people who thronged him.

Now Fate so willed it that, as he came by, Bedr-el-Budur was sitting at a window of the kiosk; and, when she heard the tumult and saw the pedlar about whom it turned, she bade her maid go and see what was the matter. The girl went, and soon returned, saying, "O my lady, it is a poor pedlar who is asking old lamps for new ones; and the people are mocking him, for without a doubt he is mad." "It seems proof enough," answered Lady Bedr-el-Budur, laughing. " 'Old wine for new' I could understand, but 'old lamps for new' is strange. Hast thou not an old lamp so that we might test him and see whether his cry be true or false?"

Now the damsel had seen an old lamp in Aladdin's apartment, and hastened to acquaint her mistress with this. "Go and bring it!" said the Lady Bedr-el-Budur, who had no knowledge whatever of the Lamp and its wonderful virtues. So the maid went and brought the Lamp, little knowing what woe she was working Aladdin. Then the Lady Bedr-el-Budur called one of the memluks and handed him the Lamp, bidding him go down to the pedlar and exchange it for a new one. Presently he returned, bearing a new lamp, and, when the Princess took it and saw that it was a far better one than the old one, she laughed and said, "Verily this man is mad! A strange trade, and one that can bring him small profit. But his cry is true, therefore take him this gold to cover his losses." And she gave the memluk ten gold pieces, and

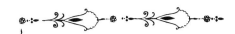

bade him hasten. But the memluk returned anon with the ten pieces, saying that the pedlar had disappeared, having left all his new lamps with the people. The Lady-Bedr-el-Budur wondered at this, but knew not, nor guessed the terrible consequences of her act.

As for the Dervish, as soon as he had got the Lamp, he recognized it. Placing it in his bosom, he left all else and ran, which to the people was only a further proof of his madness. On and on he ran, through the city and its outskirts, until he came to the desert, where at last he was alone. Then, and not till then, he took the Lamp from his bosom and rubbed it. In a flash appeared the Slave of the Lamp. "What is thy wish? I am the Slave of the Lamp which is in thy hands." And the Dervish replied, "I desire thee to take the palace of Aladdin, with all it contains, and convey it to the land of the Moors in Africa, and set it down upon the open space within the gardens of my dwelling in that land. Take me also with it. I have spoken." "O my master," said the Slave, "in the twinkling of an eye it is done. If thou carest to close thine eyes for one moment, when thou openest them thou wilt find thyself within the palace, in thy garden in the land of the Moors." And ere the Dervish could say, "I have closed my eye and opened it again," he found that it was even so, as the Slave had said. The palace and all in it were in his own garden, in his own country, with the sun of Africa shining in upon him.

Now the Lady Bedr-el-Budur was within the palace, but Aladdin was not. He had not yet returned from the chase. This thing had taken place after nightfall, so that as yet none had perceived it. But at the hour of the rising of the full moon, the Sultan looked forth from a window to admire Aladdin's palace in its silver light; what was his surprise to find that there was no palace there! All was bare and open space just as it had been before this wonderful palace was built. "By Allah!" he cried in distress and alarm. "Can it be that the Vizier was right, and that this splendid thing was but the fabric of sorcery, built in a single night and dissolved in a moment like a dream on waking? And my daughter, where is she? Oh woe! oh woe!" And the Sultan wrung his

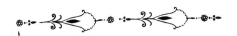

hands in grief. Then presently he summoned the Grand Vizier, and bade him look forth at the palace of Aladdin. And when the Vizier looked forth and saw no splendid edifice giving back the rays of the moon, but all as bare as it had been before, he turned to the Sultan, his face pale and twitching with excitement. "O King of the Age," he said, "doth thy Felicity now believe that the palace and all Aladdin's wealth were the work of sorcery?" And the Sultan did not reply, but beat his breast and plucked his beard; for, apart from sorcery, it was enough for him to know that Aladdin's palace was gone and his daughter with it. "Where is Aladdin?" he demanded at last in wrath. "At the chase," replied the Vizier. "Then I command thee to have him brought before me at once, pinioned and shackled."

A glad man then was the Vizier. With all alacrity he issued the Sultan's commands to the captains, who went forth with their soldiers to find and seize Aladdin. It was a difficult task for them, for they all loved him greatly; and, when they came upon him, they asked his forgiveness, yet took him and led him bound and manacled before the Sultan. But the Sultan, being filled with rage at the loss of his daughter, no sooner set eyes on Aladdin among his captors than he ordered him to the executioner. Now when this came to the ears of the people, they surrounded the palace and barred its gates and doors, and raised a great clamor without, so that the Sultan sent his Grand Vizier to ascertain the cause.

Meanwhile on the scaffold the executioner had spread the mat of death and Aladdin was kneeling thereon blindfolded, ready for the blow. The executioner walked round him thrice and then turned towards the Sultan, who stood at a window, and awaited his command to strike. At this moment the cries of the people grew louder and fiercer and the Sultan beheld them scaling the walls of the palace. Then fear got hold of him for the issue, and he signalled to the executioner to stay his hand, and bade the Vizier proclaim to the people that Aladdin was pardoned.

As soon as Aladdin was freed from his chains he begged speech of the

Sultan, and said to him, "O my lord, I thank thee for thy clemency, though I know not yet wherein my offence lay." So the Vizier took Aladdin to the window and bade him look forth. Utter amazement fell upon Aladdin when he saw that his palace had completely disappeared, leaving no vestige to mark the spot where it had stood. He was so dazed and bewildered that he turned in silence and walked back into the Sultan's presence like one in a dream. "Well," said the Sultan, "where is thy palace? And, what is more to me, where is my daughter?" And Aladdin shook his head shorrowfully and spread his hands in helpless despair; but made no other reply, for he was dumbfounded. Again the Sultan spoke: "It was my thought to set thee free so that thou mayest search for my daughter and restore her to me. For this purpose I grant thee a delay of forty days, and, if in that time thou canst not find her, then, by Allah! I will cut off thy head." And Aladdin answered him, "O King of the Age, if I find her not within forty days then I no longer wish to have a head left upon my body."

And Aladdin went forth sad and dejected. The cries of joy with which the people greeted him fell like lead on his aching heart. He escaped from their good will and wandered in the city like one distraught, greeting none, nor raising his eyes to any greeting. For two days he neither ate nor drank for grief at what had happened. Finally he wandered beyond the confines of the city into the desert. There, on the bank of a dark pool, he resolved to drown himself and so end his misery. But being devout and fearing God, he must first perform his ablutions. So he stooped and took water in his hands and rubbed them together, when lo! a strange thing happened; for as his hands came together, he chanced to rub the ring which was on one of his fingers. In a flash the Slave of the Ring appeared and standing before him, said, "O my master, what is thy desire?" Aladdin then was seized with great joy, and he cried, "O Slave, I desire my palace and my wife." "Alas!" answered the Slave, "that I cannot bring about, for this matter is protected by the Slave of the Lamp who hath put a seal upon it." "Then," urged Aladdin, "since thou canst

not bring the palace and my wife to *me*, transport *me* to the palace wherever it may be upon the earth." "On the head and the eye," replied the Slave, and immediately Aladdin found himself borne swiftly through the air and set down by his palace in the land of the Moors. Although the night had fallen he could recognize it without difficulty, and close at hand was the window of his wife's chamber. Great joy at this exhausted what little strength remained to him — for he had neither eaten nor slept for many days — and, overcome with fatigue and weakness, he threw himself down beneath a tree and slept.

Awakened at dawn by the singing of birds in the garden, Aladdin arose, and, having bathed in a stream, recited the morning prayer, after which he returned and sat beneath the window of Bedr-el-Budur's apartment. Now the Lady Bedr-el-Budur, filled with grief at her separation from her husband and her father, could neither sleep nor eat by reason of her keen distress. Each day when dawn leapt into the sky she would arise and sit at her window and weep. And on this morning she came as usual, but did not weep, for she saw Aladdin sitting on the ground outside. And they both cried out and flew to one another; and their greeting was full of joy. She opened a side door for him, bidding him enter, for she knew it was not the time for the accursed Dervish to come to see her as was his daily wont. Then, when they had embraced and kissed and shed tears of joy, Aladdin said to her, "O my beloved, before all else answer me one question: in my apartment there was an old copper lamp which —" "Alas," broke in Bedr-el-Budur, "that lamp was the cause of it all, for the man who obtained it by a stratagem told me of its virtues, and how he had achieved this thing by its aid." And immediately Aladdin heard this and he knew that it was indeed the Dervish who had worked this woe upon him.

"Tell me, how doth this accursed man treat thee?" he asked. "He cometh once a day," she replied, "and he would fain win my love and console me for thy loss, for he saith the Sultan, my father, hath struck off thy head, and at the best thou wert of poor family and stole thy wealth from him. But he gets no

word from me, only tears and lamentations." And Aladdin embraced her again and comforted her for what she had suffered. "Tell me," he asked again presently, "where doth this accursed keep the Lamp?" "Always in his bosom," she replied, "where he guards it with the greatest care and none knows of it but me." Aladdin was overjoyed when he heard this, for he thought he saw a way to obtain the Lamp. "Listen, my beloved," he said, "I will leave thee now and return shortly in disguise. Bid thy maid stand by the side door to let me in. Then I will tell thee my plan to slay this accursed one and take the Lamp."

Then Aladdin went forth upon the road that led to the city, and he had not journied far before he met a poor peasant proceeding to his daily toil. Stopping him he offered to exchange his own costly garments for those the peasant was wearing. But the man demurred, whereat Aladdin set upon him and effected the exchange by force. Then, leaving the peasant battered and bruised but dressed like a prince, he went on into the city, and, coming to the market, purchased some powder of benj, which is called "the son of an instant," for it stupefies in a moment. With this he returned to the palace, and, when he came to the side door where the maid was waiting, she recognized him and opened immediately. Very soon he was exposing his plan to Bedr-el-Budur.

"O my beloved," he said, "I wish thee to attire thyself gaily, and adorn thyself with jewels in the sparkle of which no grief can live; and, when the accursed cometh, greet him with a smile and a look from thy lovely eyes. Then invite him to sup with thee, and, when thou hast aroused a blinding passion in his bosom, he will forget the Lamp which lieth there. See," he drew forth the powder, "this is benj, the 'son of an instant.' It cannot be detected in red wine. Thou knowest the rest: pledge him in a cup and see to it that the benj is in his and not in thine. Thou canst do this?"

"Yea," replied Bedr-el-Budur. "It is difficult, but I will dare all for thee; and well I know that this accursed wretch deserves not to live." And on this assurance Aladdin withdrew to a private chamber and sat him down to wait.

He realized his extreme danger, for he knew that if the Dervish so much as suspected his existence in the flesh a rub of the Lamp and a word to the Slave would bring him instant death; but he did not know that Bedr-el-Budur, having learnt the virtues of the Lamp, had exacted a pledge from the Dervish that he would make no further use of it until she had given him her final decision as to whether she would come to him of her own free will and accord, which she maintained was a better thing than subsequently to be compelled by the abominable power of sorcery.

When the Dervish appeared, she sat weeping as usual, and it was not until, in his protestations of love, he said words that were suitable to her purpose that she paused and half dried her tears as if it needed little more to make her weigh his petition with care. Observing this he drew near and sat by her side, and now, though no longer weeping, she had not yet found words for him. He took her hand, but she snatched it away crying, "No, it cannot be! Never can I forget Aladdin!" He pleaded with her, and his passion made him eloquent. She pushed him away petulantly. "Nay, nay," she cried, "I cannot resign my heart to thee at will. Give me, I pray thee, a little space of time—I will come to thee in one hour."

So she went, leaving the Dervish in an ecstasy of doubt. At the expiration of the hour the door opened and she stood before him a vision of loveliness in resplendent attire bedecked with priceless jewels. A smile was on her face and her answer to him was in her eyes. She seated herself by his side and said boldly, "Thou seest how it is with me. My tears for Aladdin—who is dead—flowed till the hour was half spent; then, I know not why, they changed to tears of joy for thee, who art alive. Then I arose and arrayed myself gladly and came to thee. Yet even now I am not wholly thine, for tears—now grief now joy, I know not which—contend in mine eyes for him or thee. Wherefore come not too near me lest what thou hast won be forfeited. Perchance if we sup together with a jar of the red wine of thine own country—nay, go not thyself for the wine," said Bedr-el-Budur, bethinking her of the Lamp. "Do not leave me. One of my slave girls will go."

While she was gone Bedr-el-Budur pretended to busy herself issuing orders to the household about the preparation of supper. And under cover of this she sought and found Aladdin. "It is well," she said as he held her to his heart and pressed his lips to hers. "But, O my beloved," he replied, "art thou sure that the Lamp is in his bosom?" "I will go and see," she answered. And she returned to the Dervish and, approaching him shyly, began to doubt the truth of this great thing — his love for her. As she did this she placed her hands on his shoulders and looked into his eyes; whereat the Dervish drew her close to him and she felt the Lamp in his bosom. Immediately she wrenched herself free and left him with a glance in which disdain and love were kindly mixed. "It is so," she said on returning to Aladdin, "the Lamp is in his bosom, and, since he embraced me — I could not help it nor could I endure it, beloved — it is a wonder the Slave of the Lamp did not appear to see how I tore myself away, I was pressed so close."

Meanwhile the slave girl returned with the wine, and, supper being ready, Bedr-el-Budur invited the Dervish to sit by her at the table. And when they had eaten somewhat, she paused and questioned him with a glance. It was for him to call for wine, and he did so. Immediately a slave girl filled their goblets, and they drank; and another and another until the distance between them was melted, and they became, so to speak, the best of boon companions.

At length, when the supper was drawing to an end, and the wits of the Dervish were well mastered by wine, Bedr-el-Budur leaned towards him in an unbending mood. "This wine of thine has set me on fire, beloved!" she said. "But one more cup and then, if I say thee nay, do not believe me, for thou hast kept thy pledge and hast won me as man wins woman. And this shall be a loving cup, for it is the fashion in my country for the lover to take the loved one's cup and drink from it." "O lovely one of my eye," he replied, "I will honor thy custom, since thou hast so greatly honored *me*."

At this Bedr-el-Budur took his cup and filled it for herself, while a slave girl, who knew what to do as well as she hated the Dervish, handed him the cup which, though it contained the benj, she had just filled as if for her mistress. She even had to be told twice that it was not for her mistress but for the guest. So the Dervish took it, and looked into the eyes of Bedr-el-Budur brimming with love. They drank, and immediately the Dervish fell senseless at her feet, while the cup, flung from his nerveless hand, clattered across the floor.

In the space of moments Aladdin was on the spot. Bedr-el-Budur's arms were round his neck, and she was sobbing on his breast, while the Dervish lay stretched helpless before them. And when he had comforted her she went, and the slave girls with her. Then Aladdin locked the door, and, approaching the Dervish, drew the Lamp from his bosom. This done, he stood over him and swore a fearful oath, then, without further shrift, he drew his sword and hewed off his head, after which he drove the point of the sword through his heart, for only in this way can a wizard be warned off the realm of mortals.

Once in possession of the Lamp Aladdin lost no time. He rubbed it and immediately the Slave appeared. "I am here, O my master; what is thy wish?" "Thou knowest," replied Aladdin. "Bear this palace and all that is in it to the Land of Cathay and set it down on the spot from which thou didst take it at the command of that." He pointed to the dismembered wizard. "It is well," said the Slave, who served the living and not the dead; "I hear and obey, on the head and the eye." Then Aladdin returned to Bedr-el-Budur, and, in the space of one kiss of love, the palace with all therein was carried swiftly back to the original site from which it had been taken.

Now the Sultan was in a grievous mood ever since the loss of his daughter — the apple of his eye. All night long he would weep, and, arising at dawn, would look forth on the empty space where once had stood Aladdin's palace. Then his tears would flow as from a woman's eyes, for Bedr-el-Budur was very dear to him. But, when he looked forth one morning and saw the

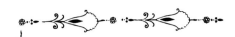 

palace standing as it had stood, he was rapt with joy. Instantly he ordered his horse, and, mounting, rode to the gates. Aladdin came out to greet him, and, taking him by the hand with never a word, led him towards the apartments of Bedr-el-Budur. She too, radiant with joy, was running to meet him. Like a bird of the air she flew to his arms, and for some moments neither of them could say a word for very happiness. Then in a torrent of words, she told him all about the accursed Dervish; how by his sorcery he had conveyed the palace to Africa, and how Aladdin had slain him, thus releasing the spell and restoring everything to its place. But not a word did she say about the Lamp and its virtues. Then they arose and went to the chamber which contained the trunk and severed head of the Dervish. And, by the Sultan's orders, these remains of the Sorcerer were burnt to ashes and scattered to the four winds of heaven.

And so Aladdin was restored to the Sultan's favor, and he and the Lady Bedr-el-Budur dwelt together in the utmost joy and happiness.

ILLUSTRATIONS

THE KING OF THE EBONY ISLES

THE MAGIC HORSE

THE WICKED HALF-BROTHERS

THE PRINCESS OF DERYABAR

ALADDIN AND THE MAGIC LAMP